"Just let me ma[ke] [it] clear," Bru growled.

"This whole *image* deal was not my idea. In case you haven't figured it out yet, you'll save yourself a lot of time and trouble by quitting now."

"Duly noted," Penelope said, hoping the quiver in her voice would go undetected by the tall Texan standing before her. "However, I have no intention of quitting."

"We'll see," he muttered, and raised his eyes to hers.

Good heavens. There ought to be a law against eyes like that, she thought, trembling. Mesmerized, Penelope had the eerie feeling that he could read her mind as a devilish half smirk, half smile stole across his lips. His lashes settled at half-mast, and he regarded her with a look that rendered her incapable of breathing. Never had a man affected her this way before. Infuriated her. Antagonized her. Interested her. Attracted her.

But Penelope knew the chances that Bru was even aware of her as anything besides a past reminder of a prim schoolmarm were slim to none.

Dear Reader,

This month, Silhouette Romance has six irresistible, emotional and heartwarming love stories for you, starting with our FABULOUS FATHERS title, *Wanted: One Son* by Laurie Paige. Deputy sheriff Nick Dorelli had watched the woman he loved marry another and have that man's child. But now, mother and child need Nick. Next is *The Bride Price* by bestselling author Suzanne Carey. Kyra Martin has fuzzy memories of having just married her Navajo ex-fiancé in a traditional wedding ceremony. And when she discovers she's expecting his child, she knows her dream was not only real...but had mysteriously come true! We also have two not-to-be missed new miniseries starting this month, beginning with *Miss Prim's Untamable Cowboy*, book 1 of THE BRUBAKER BRIDES by Carolyn Zane. A prim image consultant tries to tame a very masculine working-class wrangler into the true Texas millionaire tycoon he really is. Good luck, Miss Prim!

In *Only Bachelors Need Apply* by Charlotte Maclay, a man-shy woman's handsome new neighbor has some secrets that will make her the happiest woman in the world, and in *The Tycoon and the Townie* by Elizabeth Lane, a struggling waitress from the wrong side of the tracks is romanced by a handsome, wealthy bachelor. Finally, our other new miniseries, ROYAL WEDDINGS by Lisa Kaye Laurel. The lovely caretaker of a royal castle finds herself a prince's bride-to-be during a ball...with high hopes for happily ever after in *The Prince's Bride*.

I hope you enjoy all six of Silhouette Romance's terrific novels this month...and every month.

Regards,

Melissa Senate,
Senior Editor

Please address questions and book requests to:
Silhouette Reader Service
U.S.: 3010 Walden Ave., P.O. Box 1325, Buffalo, NY 14269
Canadian: P.O. Box 609, Fort Erie, Ont. L2A 5X3

MISS PRIM'S UNTAMABLE COWBOY

Carolyn Zane

Silhouette

ROMANCE™

Published by Silhouette Books

America's Publisher of Contemporary Romance

For my witty, elegant, intelligent, thoughtful, generous—not
to mention *beautiful*—cousin, Grace, who, when she does
not have her nose buried in a book (or a sale rack) helps me
brainstorm. And, of course, to the good Lord, for my family.
Thank you Gayle Vancil and Jan Daugherty, two real-
life Texas ranchwomen, married to two real-life Texas
cowboys.... Sigh. Thank you so much for your time
and expertise.

SILHOUETTE BOOKS

ISBN 0-373-19248-7

MISS PRIM'S UNTAMABLE COWBOY

Copyright © 1997 by Carolyn Suzanne Pizzuti

Printed in U.S.A.

Books by Carolyn Zane

Silhouette Romance

Yours Truly

*Sister Switch
†The Brubaker Brides
**Daddy Knows Last

CAROLYN ZANE

lives with her husband, Matt, and toddler daughter Madeline, in the scenic, rolling countryside near Portland, Oregon's Willamette River. Like Chevy Chase's character in the movie *Funny Farm*, Carolyn finally decided to trade in a decade of city dwelling and producing local television commercials, for the quaint, country life of a novelist. And, even though they have bitten off decidedly more than they can chew in the remodeling of their hundred-plus-year-old farmhouse, life is somewhat saner for her than for poor Chevy. The neighbors are friendly, the mail carrier actually stops at the box and the dog, Bob Barker, sticks close to home.

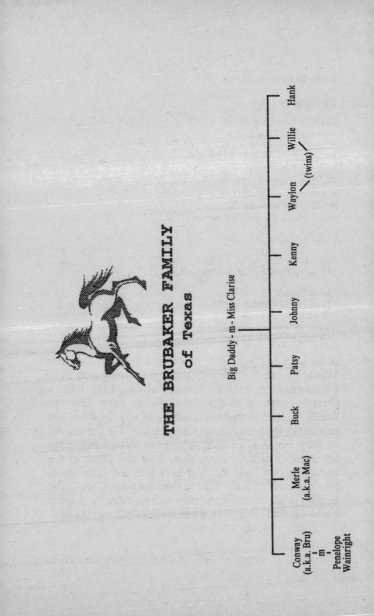

THE BRUBAKER FAMILY
of Texas

Big Daddy - m - Miss Clarise

Conway (a.k.a. Bru) — m — Penelope Wainright Merle (a.k.a. Mac) Buck Patsy Johnny Kenny Waylon Willie Hank

(twins)

Prologue

"That does it!" Big Daddy Brubaker thundered, smoke belching in furious puffs from his after-dinner cigar. "We've gotta do somethin' about gettin' these boys of ours hitched."

Much to his annoyance, Big Daddy's nine rambunctious offspring had just descended on the evening meal like a swarm of locusts, devouring everything but the pattern on the china. Then, pushing away from the table amid much hollering and shoving, they'd swarmed out of the opulent room with nary a backward glance. Arching a disgusted brow, the diminutive patriarch of this exuberant family scowled down the endless expanse of the dining room table. There, seated at the far end of the highly polished mahogany, was his wife of over thirty years, Miss Clarise.

Nodding, she blotted her lips on a linen napkin and remained silent as her husband continued to vent his frustration.

"I'm sick to death of 'em running around heah like a pack of lone wolves..."

Miss Clarise frowned, deciding to puzzle over that analogy later.

"...playin' ranch hand during the week and then turning around and playin' the field on weekends," Big Daddy groused. "Especially Bru. Being the oldest and all, he should be settin' an example. I know he's carrying on this way just to bug me. Well, I'm outa patience. I want him back at the helm of Brubaker International, where he belongs. This little rebellion of his has gone on long enough."

"Yes, Big Daddy." She sighed. "I guess it's probably time."

"It's *past* time!" he roared, pounding his fist on the mahogany to emphasize his point. "Why, Bru's pushin' thirty! When I was his age, I was already in business for myself and married to the prettiest gal in Texas."

Miss Clarise colored girlishly.

"I'm to blame, honey pie," Big Daddy lamented, sagging back against his chair. His head was barely visible above the tabletop as he eyed his equally tiny wife. "I told him to run the place, and when he did...well, okay, I admit, I interfered. But, dagnabbit anyway!" He slapped his forehead with the palm of his hand and searched the magnificent ceiling for answers. "I'm heah to tell you, puddin' cheeks—even though he did a great job for two years, it was nigh on impossible for me to back off after so many years of building an empire and let a virtual kid run everything. Ahhh..." He sighed noisily. "...well. I'm ready now. Runnin' the business just ain't the thrill it used to be."

Miss Clarise studied her husband in mild surprise. He sounded truly ready to let Bru take over again. Three years ago, she'd known how hard it was for Big Daddy to stay away from the Dallas offices and let Bru do his job. Was he finally serious about retirement?

"You know what the ironical thing is?" he asked, puffing energetic smoke rings into an intricate design. "Even though Bru handles situations differently than I would, when it comes to business, he's got the Midas touch. A natural-born leader.''

"Just like you, Big Daddy," Miss Clarise murmured.

And therein lay the problem, she was sure. Her eldest son, Conway, who was referred to as Bru by anyone who wanted to keep their front teeth, and his father were two of the most talented, hardworking, hardheaded, intelligent men she'd ever known. It was no wonder they more than occasionally clashed. Secretly, Miss Clarise felt Bru had been right to walk off the job until Big Daddy was ready to retire and hand over the reins once and for all. Certainly the continuing power struggle would have lead to a rift between her son and husband that might never have healed. Yes, back then, she'd had to give Bru credit for wisdom far beyond his twenty-six years. Under the circumstances, he'd made the only choice possible. And she knew it had been harder on him than he'd ever admit. But he'd done it because he loved his father.

Big Daddy harrumphed. "I've let this little rebellion game go on for three years, and now he's spoiled rotten. His brothers are just as bad. Not one of 'em seems to care a fig for runnin' one of my little companies anymore.''

He looked suddenly so forlorn that Miss Clarise felt mirth well up in her throat. Big Daddy always had had a flare for the dramatic. Even so, he was right. Every single one of their nine children was independent in his or her own way. And because they believed their father wasn't really as ready to retire, as he claimed, the three oldest sons—Bru, Mac and Buck—had avoided stepping into their waiting positions with Brubaker International, preferring to work the giant ranch for a while instead. They all understood that there was time enough in the future to sit behind a desk and run the show. But for now, anyway, they were young and hearty and more interested in the strong backs, deep sleep and freedom that came from hard labor on the ranch.

"Yeah," Big Daddy blustered. "They work hard. And they play hard. It's ridiculous. I'm beginning to think none of 'em is evah gonna settle down. And should we be surprised? Those three are all still wilder than March hares. What little gal in her right mind would want any of 'em? Theah nowhere near husband material."

"That's true." Miss Clarise had to agree that she didn't always approve of her sons' freewheeling lifestyles.

To Big Daddy Brubaker, nothing was more sacred than family. It was very important to him that each of his offspring find the love and happiness that he'd found with Miss Clarise. He had nine children in all: Conway, who'd always answered to Bru; Merle, whom everyone had dubbed Mac; Buck, Patsy, Johnny, Kenny, the twins Waylon and Willie and, last but most certainly not least, young Hank. Much to their eternal chagrin, Big Daddy had insisted on naming all of his children for country music stars. For if there was one thing that Big Daddy enjoyed nearly as much as he enjoyed his family, it was country music.

However, country music aside, everything else in Big Daddy's life paled in comparison to the importance of his family, including his billion-dollar bank account, his rambling antebellum mansion, known as the Circle B.O.—for Brubaker Oil—his thousands of acres of Texas ranch land, his half-dozen subsidiary companies or his many productive oil fields.

"Well, I'm tired of sittin' around waitin' for one of 'em to fall in love and tie the knot and give us a couple grandkids. This wait-and-see crap, pardon my French, just ain't my style, sugar lips," he ranted, on an impatient expulsion of cigar smoke. He waved his stubby arms, and pursed his lips into a thoughtful wad. "You know what I'm gonna do?" he asked, sitting up straight, suddenly excited as inspiration struck.

Miss Clarise tensed. "No…"

"I'm gonna take this little matter on as a…well, as a project. A mission." His jaw set in determination, he squinted across the palatial dining room at his wife. "Startin' with Bru. I'm gonna do what has to be done to get him back to work as president and CEO of Brubaker International. While I'm at it, I think I'll work on gettin' all three of the oldest boys married to some nice girls. Yep, Mac and Buck could use a kick in the pants too."

Miss Clarise could see the wheels of ambition turning in her husband's head, and felt a surge of trepidation for her three strappingly handsome eldest sons. Surely they simply needed a little more time to settle down. To mellow. Surely they would do it without their father's help.

"What...has to be done?" she asked, unable to keep the dubious note out of her voice. Even though these sons were full-grown men, and more than capable of taking care of themselves, she harbored a protective streak toward them as wide as the Lone Star State.

"I ain't exactly figured that part out yet," Big Daddy said, with a wide, rubbery grin. "But this much is for sure, those boys of ours ain't gonna know what hit 'em."

Chapter One

Penelope Grace Wainright pulled her compact car into the parking area just off the grandiose entry gate to the Circle B.O.'s formally manicured gardens. Cutting the engine, she unbuckled her safety belt and squinted through the summer sunshine at the impressive Brubaker estate, which loomed directly before her.

The huge antebellum mansion was breathtaking. Pillars, like sturdy sentinels, guarded the house proper, supporting what looked to Penelope like acres of veranda on the first and second floors. The fantastically long driveway was lined with shade trees and a half-dozen other buildings dotted the surrounding area. From where she sat peering out the windshield, Penelope could see the servants' quarters, a giant garage, the pool house, a gazebo, a greenhouse and the stables.

She smiled in satisfaction. Certainly, this would be one of her easier assignments. Why, without a doubt, anyone who lived in such luxury hardly needed to be coached in the matter of image. But who was she to dictate how the fabulously wealthy threw their money away? She was simply there to teach.

And, she thought resignedly, to collect her much-needed paycheck.

Reaching into her glove compartment, Penelope extracted a pile of inexpensive silk-type scarves, selected one, looped it around her neck and proceeded to knot it primly at her throat. Even though the early-morning sun was already blazing-hot, in her line of work a professional demeanor was called for at all times. Smoothing the seat belt creases from her summer blazer, she took a deep breath and adjusted the rearview mirror for a quick application of lipstick.

She wished she had the funds to keep her hair in one of those short—yet chic—businesslike hairstyles. However, her ailing mother needed all of her daughter's extra spending money to pay the medical bills and to keep Penelope's younger brother, Randy, in braces and baseball shoes. So she wore her wavy sandy hair long, and kept it swept into a tidy pile at the nape of her neck. She patted this simple bun now, pushing a wispy strand into its proper place and, with a quick inspection of her straight, pearly-white teeth for lipstick, declared herself at last ready to tackle her assignment.

Big Daddy Brubaker had called her earlier in the week and offered her a fantastic amount of money to move in with his family for the summer and work on a few "image-related issues." The man's booming voice had thundered over the lines, informing her that he'd heard excellent reports about the Wainright Image Consulting firm, and he wanted the best. He'd been somewhat evasive about the exact nature of what he referred to as a "project" on the phone, but he had enthusiastically assured her that there would be a huge bonus waiting for her in September, if she was able to meet the "challenge" over the course of the summer.

No problem, she'd assured him. Penelope was an expert

at winning friends and influencing people. And the September bonus would certainly help when it came to paying for Randy's school extras.

Although, why Mr. Brubaker thought it necessary for her to actually *move into* his house was beyond her. Thank heaven for her mother's sister, Aunt Geraldine. Her generous offer to come and stay for the summer and look after her wheelchair-bound mother and her little brother had enabled Penelope to take this position without worry.

Yes. This was definitely a first in her short but successful career as an image consultant. However, he was the employer here—eccentric or not—and she wouldn't question the logic behind this decision. She only knew that she would try to enjoy her brief foray into the lifestyles of the rich and famous, polish whatever rough edges needed smoothing for Mr. Brubaker's project and be on her way.

Piece of cake, she thought smugly, and reached to adjust her rearview mirror back to its original position. Her fingertips hovered at the rim as her eye was caught by a puff of smoke behind her car. Twisting around in her seat, Penelope glanced through the car's rear window.

In a quick double take, her eyes widened fearfully when she discovered that the puff of smoke was actually a dusty wake, kicked up by a pickup truck as it tore at breakneck speed down the magnificent driveway. From where she sat, it appeared to be aimed directly at her.

Before she knew what was happening, this runaway rocket careened out of control into the parking area where she sat, suddenly frozen stiff. With an ear-splitting squeal, the bright red four-wheel-drive pickup truck skidded a hundred and eighty degrees and came to a bouncing halt mere inches from her car door.

Penelope's heart thundered savagely beneath her button-down blouse, and she covered her mouth to stifle a scream of terror. Surely, she thought with a surge of righteous indignation as she sat clutching at the scarf at her throat, the maniac who piloted this vehicle had a death wish. Feel-

ing as winded as if she'd just run a mile, Penelope gasped
for air and thanked her lucky stars that she was still alive.

The maniac in question tumbled out of the shiny red
driver's-side door and landed in a lanky heap on the
ground. He sat there for a moment, blinking into the morning sunlight, then finally gathered his wits and, with a
shake of his head, clutched the truck's running board and
hauled himself to a standing position. Reaching for his
cowboy hat, he beat it on his thigh to rid it of excess dust,
then crammed it on his silky blond head. He stomped his
cowboy boots on the ground, as if to get the blood circu-
lating, then, pushing off the still-open door of his truck,
swaggered—Penelope could think of no other word to describe his easy, leggy gate—toward the house.

His hands rested at his lower back as he paused for a
moment to stretch. With a mighty yawn, he glanced back
over his shoulder, as if he could feel her presence, and
then, spotting her still sitting frozen in her seat, grinned.
It was the kind of lazy, insolent, lopsided grin that started
at one dimpled cheek and spread across his sun-kissed
face, pushing deep crevices to bracket his smirking lips.
He tapped the brim of his hat in a salute of sorts, then
turning his back on her, continued to swagger toward the
house.

Penelope sat for a moment, too stunned to move. Good
heavens. Did all the ranch hands act in such an obnoxious
manner? It was a wonder that Big Daddy didn't fire such
a lawless miscreant. And, after terrifying her half out of
her wits, to patronize her so rudely... Just who did he think
he was? Pressing her nose to the window, Penelope wondered how on earth she was supposed to open her door.
That rebel of a ranch hand had left only inches between
the tailgate of his truck and her car. She glanced at her
watch. A few more minutes, and she would be late.

Penelope Wainright was never late.

With a disgusted sigh, she hiked the skirt of her tailored

suit up high on her thighs and crawled toward the passenger door.

Bru "nobody calls me Conway" Brubaker poured himself a cup of coffee from the pot that Chef had left on the drainboard for stragglers such as himself. *Man,* he thought, tossing his Stetson on the table and plowing a hand through his thick, still-uncombed hair, *he had to stop partying on Sunday nights.* He was getting too old to dance till dawn down at The Jubilee Truckstop anymore.

Groaning audibly, he ambled toward the kitchen window and stared unseeing out into the parking area near the gate. The coffee burned a trail down his throat as he attempted to kick-start his day. Criminy. He should have known better. Now he'd be half-asleep for the better part of the morning. Lucky thing his horse had gotten a decent night's sleep. At least that way someone would be on the job. Running a hand across the sandy stubble that graced his squarish jaw, Bru sighed and peered blearily through the window at his truck.

He'd left the door open. The keys were most likely still hanging in the ignition, too.

Big Daddy was probably right, Bru grudgingly admitted as he took another scalding swig of java. Maybe it was time to grow up. After all, he thought, his mood as black as the circles that shadowed his eyes, if he kept on at this pace, he'd be dead by forty, and he seriously doubted the pearly gates would be beckoning.

He grimaced. His temples throbbed, his gut ached, and his feet were killing him. What the heck month was it? June? Well, come January, he was making a New Year's resolution. No more parties. That whole scene was getting old, anyway. It was time to straighten up and fly right again. Probably should start searching for that wife Big Daddy was always harping on…. He pushed his fingertips into the pain that radiated from his temple. Man. He really must be feeling guilty. Blowing into his cup, Bru rethought the marriage issue.

"Nah," he whispered. Maybe he'd wait on that awhile longer. He liked being a bachelor too much. No woman running around telling him what to do all the time. Making sure his socks matched, and the like. Yeah, for now, he'd just work on toning down his social life.

Rubbing his eyes, Bru blinked and swung his gaze to the other side of his truck. What on earth was that woman out in the parking lot doing? he wondered, a grin slowly chasing the scowl from his face. One shapely leg at a time, she emerged from her car window. It would seem that she'd parked too close to the fence on the passenger side and he'd hemmed her in on the driver's side.

He couldn't really have said he was sorry, given the view.

He might be half blind from last night's wine, women and song, but even half blind he could see that she had a pretty hot set of gams. Her skirt was hitched clear up to Canada, affording him a great view. Leaning against the glass, he angled his head to follow her progress.

Who was she? he wondered. Wasn't often that a business-type woman like her arrived bright and early on a Monday morning out here at the ranch. Once she'd landed on solid ground and pushed her clothing back into place, Bru could see that she was wearing a persnickety business suit and a fussy little scarf knotted into an annoying bow at her throat. He had the strangest urge to run outside and mess up her tidy little bun and pull off that ridiculous scarf and jacket.

Something about little Miss Priss and her upwardly mobile briefcase went against the grain at this stage of his postparty recovery. The coffee cup rested forgotten in his hand as he watched her stride purposefully toward the house, donning her glasses, pushing them up on her nose and checking her watch as she went. That reminded him— he'd better get to work.

"Bru?"

"Hmm?" he asked, turning toward the sound of his mother's voice as she poked her head through the kitchen's swinging door.

"Big Daddy would like to see you for a moment in the library, as soon as you're done with your breakfast," she said with a smile, her soft voice sending a pang of guilt zinging through his gut. Miss Clarise had made it clear on many occasions that she did not approve of her oldest son's rather decadent lifestyle of late.

Responding to the slight note of parental censure in her voice, he sighed. "Did he say what it was about?"

"You'll have to ask him all the details, honey, but it has to do with some plans he's making for your future. Buck and Mac's, too," she added. "And, Bru? Please hear him out."

A muscle jumped in his jaw. More plans for the future, huh? When would Big Daddy ever give it a rest? Closing his eyes, Bru counted ten pulsing beats as his head throbbed in pain. Just what he needed. More of Big Daddy's high-pressure career counseling. It wouldn't be the first time. He knew it wouldn't be the last. At least his brothers had to be there, too. With a Herculean effort, he opened his eyes and smiled at his mother.

"Yes, ma'am," Bru said. Miss Clarise was a southern lady in every sense of the word. Refined, sophisticated, gentle and loving. His father was so lucky to have her. They didn't make 'em like Miss Clarise anymore. At least not that Bru was able to see. "Tell him I'll be along in a minute."

Her sparkly eyes crinkled at the corners. "I'll tell him." The kitchen door hushed shut, and Miss Clarise was gone.

"Ah, brother," Bru groaned, dragging a hand across his mouth. "Why me?" he muttered. Wincing, he set his cup down and searched the multitude of Chef's cupboards for a bottle of aspirin. He was in no mood for one of Big Daddy's lectures.

* * *

Big Daddy Brubaker rushed across the library's hard-wood floor, the furious clomping of his pint-size cowboy boots echoing throughout the room. "Miz Wainright?" he thundered, extending his hand and, after giving hers a vigorous pumping, tugged her into the book-lined baronial library.

"Yes, sir," Penelope breathed, taking in the elegant surroundings as the man guided her toward an oversize wine-colored leather wingback chair. What on earth could a man like Mr. Brubaker need in the way of image consulting? she wondered in awe. Everything from the lush velvet draperies to the polished brass andirons simply screamed class.

And, as far as first impressions went, Mr. Brubaker oozed something so charming and lovable that Penelope immediately felt as if she'd stepped into the bosom of her own long-lost family. So, what was she doing here? Settling into her seat, she bestowed on Big Daddy her most cultivated, businesslike smile.

"Can I get you anything?" he boomed, hovering at her elbow. "Orange juice? Coffee? A couple farm-fresh eggs and a porterhouse steak?"

"Oh," Penelope said demurely. She rarely ate more than a muffin for breakfast. "No, thank you, Mr. Brubaker."

"Call me Big Daddy," he boomed, hoisting himself into the wingback chair opposite hers, and allowed his feet to swing boyishly. "Everyone does."

"Okay, uh, Big Daddy," Penelope said. That name would take some getting used to, she decided, as he was neither big nor her daddy. "So," she began conversationally, "what exactly did you have in mind, as far as my participation in your…project?" She looked at him expectantly.

"Miz Wainright…" he began.

"Penelope, please," she interjected.

"Well, now, that's a tricky mouthful." He grinned. "But it suits a pretty gal like you."

Penelope felt a warm glow steal into her cheeks. This man already had the tools of a successful personality down pat. "Thank you," she murmured.

"Anywho…" Big Daddy sighed and pulled a tiny booted foot up onto his opposite knee. "I got a problem that I need your help with." His raisinlike eyes were lined with worry.

Penelope frowned. "What kind of a problem?"

"My boys. Wilder than a pack of scrappin' jackals, and twice as rough around the edges."

"Your…boys?"

"Eh-yep. Not all of 'em. Just the three oldest ones. I need y'all to bust 'em in the chops, whip 'em into shape and turn 'em into businessmen, and maybe something a nice woman might be inclined to marry someday."

"Marry?"

"Eh-yep. I'm sick of lookin' at 'em across the dinner table every night. I want 'em outa heah, and under their own roofs, workin' on a few grandbabies I can bounce on my knee." He slapped his minuscule lap to emphasize his point.

Scrapping jackals? Grandbabies? Penelope swallowed. Perhaps she should reevaluate the difficulty of this project.

Big Daddy leaned forward in a confidential manner. "All they evah care about these days is tendin' the ranch. Which is fine, I reckon, but what about gettin' back to the *real* business? Brubaker International. That's all they used to want. Not anymore."

Penelope nibbled her upper lip. "No?"

"No. They're all on some kinda workers' strike, choosin' to run the ranch instead of my empire until I promise to quit interferin' for good and retire. Well, okay then. I promise. But I demand some changes on their part, too. First off, I'm disgusted with their unpolished mannahs and rowdy behavior. Bru, my eldest, is the worst. No self-

respectin' company would evah want to do business with
Brubaker International with a reprobate like him at the
helm. Since he walked out three years ago, he's gone to
pot. He used to have promise, but now, I'm beginnin' to
wonder. Out all hours, partyin' and womanizin'. Why,
that's just a bunch of crap—pardon my French, lamb chop.
And sloppy? Room's a pigsty! Well, that's no way for the
Brubaker heir apparent to behave. No woman in her right
mind would evah put up with a husband like him!'' Big
Daddy bellowed. ''So, Penelope, honey, will y'all do it?''

''Do it?''

''Will ya teach my boys some mannahs and social
skills? Start with Bru. Get him polished up real nice to run
the empire, and maybe marriage? If the lessons take with
Bru, I'll make it worth your while to stay on and tutor the
other two.''

''I...uh...'' Penelope stammered.

Before she could formulate a coherent answer, the library's doors blew open and three sandy haired, incredibly
handsome men, wearing identical scowls, strode into the
room, looking for all the world as if they were ready for
the shoot-out at the OK Corral. Legs spread, arms crossed
across broad chests, they stood in an intimidating row and
glanced from Big Daddy to Penelope and back down to
Big Daddy.

Penelope's gaze shot to the one standing in the center,
and she immediately recognized him as the driver of the
shiny red truck. Uh-oh. He wasn't a hired ranch hand.
Good heavens. He was a Brubaker. Her stomach plum-
meted, to crowd into her pumps alongside her feet. She
was supposed to polish *his* image?

''You'ah here. Good.'' Big Daddy chortled gleefully,
bounding out of his seat and gesturing grandly to the three
golden men that towered above him. ''Miz Wainright,
these are my three oldest sons. Conway, Merle and Buck.''

Penelope donned her studied mask of professionalism
and extending her hand, grasped their large, work-

roughened hands. "Merle. Buck," she said, nodding primly at each one in turn. She turned to the one who'd nearly killed her and choked, "Conway."

"Nobody calls me Conway," Bru growled.

Nonplussed, Penelope blinked at his rudeness, recoiling her hand as if he'd bitten it. Oh? And would anyone care to clue her in on His Royal Highness's moniker? she wondered, suddenly as flustered as a hen with a fox in the coop. She opened her mouth to speak, but unfortunately, no scathing words of rebuttal came to mind. An impotent squeak sounded from somewhere deep in her throat. He hadn't even said half a dozen words, and already she could tell that the man was an insufferable bore. She was a pretty good judge of character. She knew the type. Teaching him anything would be a minor miracle.

Merle and Buck tried unsuccessfully not to grin at her obvious discomfort.

"He goes by Bru," Merle volunteered. "And I answer to Mac."

"Boys!" Big Daddy roared, shifting his no-nonsense gaze up at them. "Your mother and I have come to a decision. We want you off the range and back in the boardroom where y'all belong. I've let y'all run wild long enough. 'Specially you, Bru. This here is Miz Wainright of the Wainright Image Consulting firm. I've hired her to pound some business mannahs and social skills back into your thick skulls, startin' with you, boy."

This last he directed to Conway, who Penelope now assumed preferred to be called Bru. She wished that the sky would open and a tornado would suck her out of the room and set her down in another state. Looking grouchier than a cornered bobcat after a long night of fruitless prowling, Bru's dark eyes seemed to literally laser a hole through her neatly tied scarf.

"*What?*" Bru demanded, planting his hands on his narrow hips.

"Tell 'em, honey pie," Big Daddy ordered, gesturing back to Penelope.

"Uh..." she stammered, locking her wobbly knees and smoothing her damp palms on her skirt. "I... Your father is right. I run an...image consulting firm."

"*Image consulting?*" Bru arched a suspicious brow in his father's direction, then shifted his gaze to glower at Penelope.

Gracious. A myriad of unpleasant emotions left her feeling quite daunted by this task. Never before had she encountered a client who did not wish to learn. However, she decided, taking a deep, fortifying breath in an effort to get hold of herself, she was made of sterner stuff.

Penelope Wainright never cried uncle.

"Go on," Big Daddy said encouragingly. "Tell 'em what you're gonna do."

"Well, I um... I guess we'll start at..." Her mind raced. This was such an unusual situation. Would her normal courses even apply here? "...the beginning, I guess. Lesson number one is usually learning to speak effectively. My clients tell me they've had tremendous success putting these strategies to work. Why not start there?" she suggested.

"Now you-ah talkin' honey pie!" Big Daddy rubbed his hands together. "Now, I want you boys to give this a shot. Heck, the way you're all headed, nobody's evah gonna wanna go into business with or marry a bunch of rascals like y'all. So—" he shook a menacing finger up at his three burly boys "—just do it!" He jerked his chin over his shoulder. "What time, honey pie?"

Penelope smiled weakly and lifted her shoulders. The idea of plunging into this project one-on-one with Bru was more than she could bear at the moment. For the initial meeting, anyway, she wanted his brothers there, as a buffer of sorts. Then, when she had settled in and gathered her wits, she could privately tutor the insufferable oldest Brubaker. The very idea gave her a tension headache.

"What time is breakfast served every morning?" she asked, glancing at Big Daddy.

"Chef puts out the grub at 5:00 a.m.," Big Daddy thundered. "Except Sunday. We all rest on Sunday."

"Well, okay then."

Blinking rapidly, she ignored the pain that stabbed between her eyes and forged ahead. "I usually like to get started early in the morning. For the first session, why don't we *all* get acquainted over breakfast, and then we can strategize your schedules—beginning with…er, Bru— for the individual sessions over the rest of the summer. So," she chirped, her smile bright, "why don't we meet tomorrow morning in the dining room, say 5:00 a.m.?" She looked hopefully back and forth between the three Brubaker sons. "That way, we can get to know each other and practice a little table etiquette."

"Like hell," Bru muttered, and turning on his heel, stormed out of the room.

Chapter Two

"Well, I never..." Penelope sputtered. Feeling her face burst into flame, she couldn't be sure if it was more from humiliation or from anger. She had half a mind to spin on her heel and march right out of here. But she couldn't. She was a Wainright, after all. Not to mention the fact that Big Daddy's promise of a huge bonus would solve a lot of problems for her mother and Randy.

"Oh, don't worry about him, sugar doll." Big Daddy harrumphed, watching through the library window as his oldest stalked across the driveway toward the stable. "I'll have a little talk with that one. In the meantime, why don't you get to know my other two boys? Merle here goes by Mac, and this other one...well, Buck is one of the few who actually seems to like the name I gave him." He shook his head sorrowfully. "Anywho, y'all get acquainted, okay?"

Penelope darted a dubious glance at her two latest students, summoning her flagging reserves of professionalism. "Yes, uh, okay."

The two handsome sandy-haired men looked at each

other, then shrugged in resignation. Appearing to figure that it was easier—for the moment anyway—to join Big Daddy than to beat him, they grinned at her and inclined their heads. They were each at least a foot taller than their father, lanky and lean, and, wearing faded denim and leather, appeared to be born to ranch life.

Big Daddy wagged a threatening finger at his sons. "You boys take Miz Wainright up to her room. And I expect y'all to be on your best behavior. Whatever *that* is," he muttered to himself. To Penelope he said, "I'll have Bru fetch your belongings from your car, and bring 'em up to y'all."

"Oh, I'm sure that won't be necessary," she said demurely, not wanting to further aggravate Big Daddy's rather volatile oldest son. "I only have two bags. I am more than capable of carrying them myself." She pushed her lips up at the corners, hoping to create a serene facade. The last thing she wanted was to spend any moments that were not absolutely necessary in the presence of Bru Brubaker.

"Why, I wouldn't dream of letting a little lady like y'all fend for yourself when Bru will be only too happy to take care of you." Big Daddy was vehement on the matter, and flapping his arms so that the fringe on his leather jacket danced wildly, he proceeded to shoo them out of the library.

"Well, okay then," Penelope said, hustling to keep up with the lanky strides of Bru's brothers as they led her toward one end of the elegant double staircase.

"Miz Wainright, is your car open?" Big Daddy asked as he bounded across the black-and-white marble checkerboard that sprawled endlessly throughout the vast foyer.

Penelope paused in her tracks and pulled her cheeks between her teeth to stifle a grin as she recalled her vehicle's parking situation. "Yes, sir," she nodded pleasantly. "Please tell Bru that my bags are in the back seat. The doors are all unlocked."

* * *

"This is the place," Mac said, and pushed open the double doors leading to the suite that Penelope would be occupying for the rest of the summer.

As she entered on Buck's heels, her jaw dropped and she stared in awe at the tastefully decorated room, with an adjoining bath and a spacious walk-in closet. The fireplace supported an intricately carved marble mantel, and fresh flowers filled numerous crystal vases around the room.

"Extra towels and blankets are in that closet," Buck said, and pointed across the room. "But you don't need to worry about picking up after yourself. The maids will do that." He grinned easily. "Anything else I can get you?"

"Oh, no. Thank you," Penelope breathed, returning his smile.

"Then how about me? Can I get you anything?" Mac teased.

They were both incorrigible flirts, Penelope noted, moving her professional smile from Buck to Mac. "No. You've both been very helpful. I'm sure I'll be quite comfortable." That was an understatement. She suddenly felt like raising her arms and dancing a little jig. If these two could see the small apartment that she shared with her mother and brother, they'd surely mistake it for one of the mansion's dozens of walk-in closets.

"So, Big Daddy wants you to teach us how to talk," Mac said, with a sidelong grin at his brother.

Penelope laughed. "Oh, I imagine you already know how to talk," she said, turning to face him. "No, I'm an image consultant. Not a speech therapist, or anything like that. Learning to speak effectively in business is an important part of one's future success. Just as important as the way you dress, or the first impression you make."

"The way we dress?" Buck laughed, a teasing glint in his eye. "Miz Wainright, we're ranch hands. Shucks, it don't matter none how we talk. Or dress." He was obviously putting her on.

Penelope lifted her shoulders and let them fall. Hers was

not to reason why. She had a job to do, and she would do it. "I don't know exactly what your father has in mind in regards to each of your immediate futures, but polishing your business image can never hurt," she explained with a winsome smile. "And, since he hired me to help you with your images, I intend to do just that."

"Well, good luck, Miz Wainright," Buck said, with an amused grin at Mac. "You're gonna need it, if you plan on getting anywhere with Bru."

Just then a scowling Bru entered the doorway, and Penelope's stomach tightened. She had the unfortunate feeling that they were right.

Nodding politely, Mac and Buck turned and, brushing past their older brother, headed into the hall. Bru strode into her room and tossed her bags on her bed. Straightening, he bestowed her with his standard insolent grin.

Penelope glanced at her aged suitcases in surprise. How had he managed to get them out of her car? And so quickly? She bit her lip. Must have moved that firecracker he drove.

"So you think you're gonna polish my image, huh?" he asked her challengingly, planting his hands on his hips and staring down at her.

Suddenly the massive room seemed to shrink, and Penelope wished Buck and Mac had stayed, if for no other reason than to shield her from the belligerence that burned in his dark and brooding eyes. Taking a step back, she clasped her damp palms together and wondered why she felt as if she owed him an explanation. She was working for his father, not him. If he had a problem, he should take it up with Mr. Brubaker. She was simply following orders. Jutting her chin, she lifted her nose and eyed him coolly. "I have been hired expressly for that purpose, yes."

He scratched his chest and regarded her with an arrogant expression. "Now, can you tell me what on earth I need with a new image?" He knocked his hat back on his head a bit.

If ever anyone needed help with their image, this undisciplined beast did, Penelope thought, biting back a pithy, unprofessional comment. "Why...why..." she sputtered, "...to win friends and influence people, of course." Pursing her lips, she returned his piercing gaze. His expression plainly told her what he thought of her reason. Why did he rattle her so? Usually, Penelope was completely unflappable.

"Honey, I've got plenty of *friends*," he drawled, and arched a lazy brow. "If you catch my drift. As far as influence goes, my last name gets me into most places with no trouble. And, I *don't* need any pretentious fancified table manners, especially since I take most my meals out in the stable with the guys."

Suddenly, Penelope was mad. Spitting-mad. How dare this overgrown cowboy make fun of her chosen profession? He was trying to intimidate her. Well, he could forget that. Wainrights were never intimidated. However, his boorish behavior only served to fuel her contention that Big Daddy had been right. These well-heeled dunderheads needed her. They needed her badly. Big Daddy had also been right about this being a project. Perhaps one of the largest and most difficult she'd ever undertaken. But she was up to it.

Besides, she desperately needed the money.

"Be that as it may," Penelope snapped, crossing her arms beneath her breasts as she turned to face Bru's smirking mouth. It was too bad, she thought, as her eyes perused his face, that such good looks were wasted on such a rotten apple. "I was hired by your father to help you, and help you I shall." Her declaration echoed in the silent room.

"You can try," Bru said with an arrogant grin. Hooking his thumbs through his belt loops, he allowed his gaze to rudely appraise her for a moment before he turned abruptly on his heel and strode out of the room.

Penelope didn't know which was worse—being all alone in a room with that irritating man, or having him walk out on her without so much as a backward glance. Opening and closing her fists, she mentally counted to ten. Then twenty. Marching to the door, she called after him.

"*Mr.* Brubaker. I shall expect to see you tomorrow morning at 5:00 a.m. sharp, down in the dining room."

Bru's ribald laughter reverberated down the long hallway.

Penelope checked her watch again. Five-fifteen a.m., and still no sign of Bru. He'd managed to avoid her for the rest of the afternoon yesterday, so she'd had no chance to remind him that he was expected here at the breakfast table at 5:00 a.m. sharp. Tardiness was not acceptable. Though she was beginning to get the idea that acceptability mattered not one whit to Bru.

She glanced at her rapidly cooling eggs Benedict and wondered if Big Daddy had found time to have that chat he'd threatened with his oldest son. Though not a gambler, Penelope would have staked her September bonus on the supposition that—if it had happened yet—their little talk had not been a pleasant affair. If there was one thing that Bru seemed to have inherited from his father, it was his hard head. No one else in the rest of the family—and she'd met all but one of them over a chaotic dinner table last night—seemed nearly as obstinate as Bru.

She had enjoyed meeting the multitude of Brubaker offspring, all named for famous country singers. The only one she'd missed was Bru's sister, Patsy, who would be studying dance in Europe for the rest of the summer. Penelope envied Patsy, having so many attentive, handsome brothers to spoil her, and looked forward to someday meeting the only Brubaker daughter.

Hopefully, Patsy didn't take after her oldest brother.

Adjusting her glasses, she darted a quick look at her wrist, and bit back the urge to scream. Instead, she sent a confident, professional smile in the direction of Mac and

Buck as they sat in a bleary-eyed daze across the breakfast table from her.

"Is 5:00 a.m. too early?" she ventured, puzzled. Surely, ranch hands normally had to get up much earlier than this.

"Oh, ahhhh...no, ma'am," Buck said with a wide yawn. "We're usually up by now. In fact, most of the family and crew has most likely already eaten breakfast out in the kitchen, except for Miss Clarise and Big Daddy and some of the younger kids."

"Then why are you so tired?" came her query.

"Well, for the most part, we don't have to concentrate on all that much most mornings," Mac said, catching his brother's contagious yawn. "Just...ahhhh, you know, ridin' and ropin' and the like."

"I see." She cleared her throat. "Why don't you two study the introductory material I've provided, while I go see what's keeping your brother?" she suggested, gesturing toward the handouts that sat before them on the table.

"I wouldn't do that, Miz Wainright," Mac warned.

"Penelope, please. And why not?"

"Bru's not much of a morning person," Buck said with a sleepy grin. "Never has been. In fact, he's the only one in the family who doesn't get up with the chickens."

"Shoot," said Mac, "sometimes he don't even get up with the lunch whistle."

"I'm not concerned with his morning rituals." Penelope sighed. She was definitely not amused. "If one of you would be so kind as to show me to his room, I shall have a talk with him."

Suddenly wakeful, Mac and Buck darted a wide-eyed glance at each other. "Maybe we'd better both go," they suggested.

"Whatever." Penelope checked her watch. Time was money. "Let's go."

"Mr. Brubaker. Please come to the door." Penelope rapped on the mahogany once again, and wished it was

Bru's head. *Self-confidence*, she reminded herself. *Believe, believe, believe in yourself,* she chanted in her mind. *There is power in thinking positively. I can do this. I think I can, I think I can...* She glanced at her watch. Five twenty-five and counting. "Mr. Brubaker! I'm waiting!" She rapped once more.

"Excuse me, Miz...uh, Penelope, but that's never gonna do the trick," Buck said with a shake of his head.

"Not unless you're toting heat," Mac joshed.

They were both hovering at her elbow, enjoying the show.

Penelope bristled. "No? Well, short of 'toting heat,' would you mind telling me what does work?" She was growing more exasperated by the minute.

"I'd just give up, if I were you," Buck advised. "I'm serious as a heart attack about him not being very nice in the morning."

"As opposed to say...the afternoon?" Penelope's voice was loaded with sarcasm. She'd had enough. It was time to take this bull by the horns and roust him out. Twisting the knob, she was surprised to discover the door unlocked. She pushed it open and marched in, Buck and Mac hot on her heels.

"Mr. Brubaker! Time to rise and shine," she called at the disheveled lump that graced the middle of the king-size mattress.

Striding over to the window, she tugged on the blinds and, with a resounding snap, allowed the sun to stream into the room. Able to see her surroundings now, Penelope decided that Big Daddy had been right. Bru was a slob.

It was too bad, she thought, curiously scanning his private domain. The suite was magnificently decorated, from what she was able to tell beneath the piles of blue jeans that were strewn hither and yon. Cowboy boots were tossed haphazardly around the floor, and Western-style shirts of all colors littered the rich furnishings, along with magazines and newspapers.

Perhaps, she mused, the maids were afraid to venture across the threshold to Bru's world. Penelope couldn't say that she'd blame them.

At the sound of her voice, Bru sat bolt upright in bed and flung the covers off his head. Blanket marks creased his face, and his hair, squashed flat on one side, enhanced the fact that he was madder than a walleyed rattlesnake. He blinked angrily at the smiling trio who stood near the foot of his bed.

"What the—?" he sputtered. Was this some kind of a bad dream? His gaze swung to the yapping female.

"Mr. Brubaker. I'm sure that this is not the image of success that your father wishes you to project."

Bru scowled up at her in disbelief. *Where the heck did Big Daddy come up with this Little Mary Sunshine?* he wondered incredulously, his mouth hanging open as she looked down at him in disapproval.

"'Punctuality is the image of success,'" she quoted. "'In order to achieve one's goal, one must first project the image one wishes to attain.'"

What in tarnation was she talking about? His eyes moved to her mouth as her lips formed the words of admonishment. It sounded like English, but he'd be darned if he could follow her. Besides, the only image he cared to project at the moment was the dead-to-the-world image.

"I'll show you the image I wish to project," he growled, climbing out of bed, wearing nothing but his underwear. "How's this for an image?" he asked, pointing savagely toward his bedroom door. *"Get outa here!"*

Penelope's gaze flitted momentarily to his naked torso, then back up to his face. Bru was pleased to note the pink stain that colored her cheeks and the small puff of air that escaped from between her softly parted lips. Good. Now maybe she'd get it through her prissy little head that he had no intention of playing her image game and let him get some much-needed shut-eye.

"No, sir." Penelope stood her ground. "I have no intention of taking one step toward the door until you agree to accompany me downstairs for our introductory session. Then, after we're all a little better acquainted…''

Bru cocked his head and darted a quick glance at his brothers. Better acquainted? He'd sat buck naked in a bathtub and played battleship with these two idiots, and that had been a quarter of a century ago. How much better did he have to know them?

''…and review our schedules, you and I will plan a time to meet and begin work on lesson one, learning to speak effectively.''

Plowing a hand through his tangled hair, Bru shook his head and stared at her in amazement. Learning to speak effectively? At this hour? He could barely grunt coherently before noon on most days. He blinked at her. She was serious. Her tenaciousness boggled his mind.

And, though he desperately wanted to pick her up— floppy bow and all—and carry her out into the hallway and shut the door in her professionally smiling face, some part of him couldn't help but admire her. Something about her plucky determination reminded him of Miss Clarise. But even his mother knew better than to invade the sanctuary of his room at this hour of the morning.

Big Daddy had hit an all-time low in the department of interfering in his life. When would his father ever get it through his head that until he stopped meddling for good, Bru wasn't interested in anything but working the ranch? At least out on the range, Big Daddy couldn't watch his every move like a hawk. Out on the range, *he* was in charge. Glancing at Penelope, he snorted. Out on the range, he didn't have to speak effectively.

What on earth had Big Daddy been thinking? *Image Consulting.* Resentment filled Bru's growling, empty belly. Here he was, in his late twenties, and still being treated like some kind of wet-behind-the-ears kid. Big Daddy knew darn good and well that he was perfectly capable of running the corporation. Criminy, he'd already done it for two years. And, he'd done it well. He sighed. Big Daddy just wasn't ready to give up his precious baby yet. Okay. Fine. When the old man was ready to step down, they would talk. Until then, if and when Bru ever decided he needed help with his image, *he'd* be the one to make the arrangements. For now, anyway—for as long as Big Daddy was calling the shots—Bru was going to keep his distance.

Beginning with the persnickety Miz Wainright and her ridiculous image lessons. If he played his cards right, she'd quit before the end of the week.

"If you were planning on showering, I suggest you do so now," Penelope said with a sigh and a glance at her wristwatch. "The clock is ticking, and we have a lot of ground to cover today."

What? She was ordering him to the shower? Who *was* this woman? "Now, hold on just a darn minute," Bru barked, summoning as much dignity as he could muster, given the fact that he was wearing nothing but his underwear. "*You* don't tell *me* when to take a shower, woman."

He took a menacing step toward Penelope and, planting his hands on his hips, squinted down into her face. "In fact, you don't tell me when to do anything. I'm sick to death of being manipulated like some kind of pawn in Big Daddy's screwball chess game. I'm a ranch hand. Get it? The cattle don't care if I can speak effectively. They don't care if I can speak at all!" Bru waved his arms wildly— he was just getting warmed up.

It felt kind of good to vent his frustration. He hated treading water with his life, but what choice did he have? Until now, he hadn't realized just how much this whole situation really bugged him. Angered him. Hurt him.

Come to think of it, he was furious.

"And another blasted thing! Whose bright idea were table etiquette lessons? I don't need to know which fork goes with the salad. Out on the range, it ain't no Martha Stewart picnic, got that? We eat beans on a tin plate—"

okay, that was a creative exaggeration, but man, it felt good to get this off his chest "—with a *spoon!*" He glared at her, a challenge in his eyes, and suddenly heard what he was saying. Dragging a fist over his jaw, he realized he was beginning to sound like his father. "Augghh." He groaned out loud.

Penelope touched her lower lip with the tip of her tongue, and took a shaky step backward.

Mac motioned for Buck to move around the bed and said, "Come on, Buck, old buddy. I can see that Bru has gotten up on the wrong side of the bed."

Buck sighed in agreement. "Again."

Together, they each grabbed for one of Bru's arms and pulled him toward the edge of the bed. Then they practically dragged the sputtering Bru onto his feet and across the room and shoved him into the bathroom. Before the eldest Brubaker could turn around, Mac and Buck slammed the bathroom door shut and wedged a chair underneath the doorknob.

Both brothers leaned their backs against the door frame, crossed their arms and grinned wickedly.

"Don't you worry, ma'am," Buck said to a startled Penelope. "We won't let him out until he's cleaned up and eager to get down to breakfast."

Mac spoke up over the indignant howls and shouts of outrage behind the bathroom door, "He's always a lot nicer after his morning shower," he told Penelope with a quick, reassuring nod.

She sighed. "I'm counting on that."

On their way downstairs to begin their day, Big Daddy and Miss Clarise paused outside their oldest son's door and listened to the thumping and hollering.

"My land!" Miss Clarise exclaimed.

"Sounds like Miz Wainright started polishin' Bru's image this mornin'." Big Daddy chortled and threw a companionable arm around his wife's slender shoulders. "I have a feelin' she's gonna work out just fine."

Chapter Three

Penelope glanced up with trepidation, as Bru—his hair still damp from the impromptu shower—stormed into the dining room, escorted on either side by a younger brother.

"Just let me make one thing perfectly clear," he growled, roughly shrugging his siblings off. "This whole...*image* deal is not my idea, and, just in case you haven't figured it out yet, you'll save yourself a lot of time and trouble by quitting while you're ahead." He crossed his arms over his chest, his stance wide, as he paused just inside the columned arch, a rugged contrast to the room's luxurious decor.

"Duly noted," Penelope said benignly, hoping the quaver in her voice was going undetected by the three men who loomed in the doorway. "However, I have no intention of quitting."

"We'll see," he muttered under his breath.

"Shall we begin?" Penelope asked, and motioned for them to take a seat at the table. *Project the image you wish to attain,* she reminded herself, and took a deep, fortifying breath.

Buck and Mac took the chairs situated on either side of Penelope. Bru moved to the opposite end of the massive table. Grabbing a chair, he turned it around, stuffed it rebelliously between his legs and seated himself with a thud.

Ignore him, Penelope told herself.

But it was hard.

Bru's mere presence had every nerve ending in her body on edge and jangling with an awareness of the negative force that radiated from the other end of the room. Her breath came in shallow, nervous puffs, her heart pounded a furious timpani in her ears. And, though she tried not to look directly at him, she could feel his piercing gaze following every move she made.

Ignore him, she told herself again.

"Generally," she said, and cleared her throat, "I, uh, like to begin each of my first sessions with introductions. But," she continued, and forced a small laugh, "since you already know each other, I thought I'd try something a little different to help me get to know you."

Although, she thought—feeling a little disgusted with herself—why she'd want to get to know Bru any better was beyond her. But, curiously enough, she did.

"So, why don't we begin by having one of you, it doesn't matter who, tell me a little bit about one of the other two. That way, I can get an objective opinion." She attempted a small, genial laugh to put them all at ease, but was disappointed at the hollow results that squeaked past her lips. Squaring her shoulders, she pushed her reading glasses higher on her nose and glanced around at her three less-than-enthusiastic students. "Who would like to begin?" she asked with a brave smile.

Mac shrugged. "I will." He shot a mischievous look down the long table at Bru. "Since Bru's the firstborn, I guess I'll tell you about him."

Penelope schooled her face into a mask of casual interest, hoping to disguise the sudden leap in her heart that sent a telltale flush cascading into her cheeks. "That would be fine, Mac. Please, go ahead."

Thunderclouds began to gather down at the other end of the room. Leaning forward on two legs of his chair, Bru zeroed his black gaze in on Mac.

"Well," Mac drawled, pulling his lower lip into his mouth and pretending to ponder this assignment, "let's see... I guess if anyone had to think up one word to describe our big brother, it would be...party animal. Oh, pardon me, ma'am. That's two words, isn't it? Well, anyway, right now Bru has kind of a playboy image. Fast cars, fast women and fast..."

The hind legs of Bru's chair thudded to the floor, causing Penelope to jump. "Can it, brother." He gritted out the words through a tightly clenched jaw.

"Excuse me, uh, Mac," Penelope put in, with a quick glance down the table at Bru's dark expression. "Perhaps you could tell us about his career goals?"

"Sure." Mac grinned. "None."

Bru's scowl at his gleeful sibling deepened, and Penelope began to fear for Mac's safety. She made another unsuccessful attempt at some light laughter, hoping to diffuse the tension she felt building but didn't quite know how to handle. This was a first for her. Mind racing, she racked her brain for her usual tidbits on how to keep social situations smooth and pleasant, and came up blank. Perhaps Dale Carnegie had never run into the likes of Bru Brubaker.

"None?" she asked. "Ah...ah...ah... Oh, surely, that can't be true."

Mac shrugged. "Ma'am, I mean no disrespect when I tell you that he doesn't need any. Any time Bru wants to step back into his seat as president and CEO of Brubaker International, all he has to do is whistle. Bru ran the entire corporation for two years awhile back. Made money hand over fist. You probably saw him on the cover of *News-*

week? A few years back they did a story on the top twenty-five businessmen in the world.''

Penelope nodded, remembering the story. That was *him* on the cover? She darted a quick peek at the brooding Bru. Amazing.

''Well, anyway, Big Daddy couldn't seem to keep his fingers out of the pie, and managed to interfere with more than one of Bru's—'' Mac rolled his eyes. ''I hate to use this word in reference to him, but what the heck—brilliant mergers. We all knew Big Daddy wasn't ready for retirement back then. Even though he wanted his firstborn to step into his place, Big Daddy just couldn't stand watching someone else do his job as well as he could.'' He chuckled. ''Big Daddy can be kind of a control freak. But that was several years ago.'' Mac looked down the table at Bru and shrugged. ''Maybe things have changed.''

Bru snorted and studied his boots, a skeptical smirk tugging at his upper lip. Penelope chanced another quick glance in his direction. At least he was listening. That was a start.

''Go on,'' she said encouragingly to Mac.

''Anyway, three years ago, Bru stepped down in the interest of family harmony. Told Big Daddy to holler when he was ready to retire for good. And Big Daddy's been hollerin' ever since. 'Course, we all know he's not serious. That's why we run the ranch. And, honest, Miz Wainright, contrary to popular belief, we're not the heathens he makes us out to be. Well,'' he recanted slightly, ''at least Buck and I aren't.''

Grinning at Bru, he stretched his arms over his head and continued, ''For now, anyway, we all enjoy our jobs working the ranch. Roping a steer takes the kind of skill Big Daddy can't hand us on a platter. I don't think he's figured that out about us yet. And Bru here, well, he's the best. Big Daddy couldn't ask for a better foreman.''

Mac dropped his arms and looked down the table, a genuine and reverent respect for his brother's talent shining in his eyes. "Ropin', shootin', ridin', whatever, I'm not kiddin' at all, ma'am, when I tell you around these parts, anyway, he can't be beat. He works harder than any of us. Guess that's why he parties so hard. Right, Bru?"

Only the muscles that jumped in Bru's jaw gave any indication at all that he even heard his brother's glowing praise. Averting her eyes from the stormy end of the table, Penelope straightened the stack of handouts beneath her fingertips, and smiled brightly at Mac.

"Well, uh, okay. Thank you, Mac." She turned to Buck. "Buck, why don't you tell me about Mac?"

"Yes, ma'am," Buck said with an affable shrug.

As Buck went on to acquaint her with his brother, Penelope found that she was unable to concentrate on a single word he said. Nodding and smiling at what she hoped were appropriate intervals, she tried to gather the gist of his introduction and store it in her brain for future reference, but it was impossible.

As if in a trance, she allowed her gaze to stray from Buck as he spoke. Slowly, very, very slowly, her recalcitrant eyes traveled of their own volition from chair to mahogany chair, until they reached the far end of the table, where Bru sat.

When she lifted her lashes, her gaze slammed into his with a collision so forceful, she felt as if she had stepped into a wind tunnel and been swept, chair and all, into the depths of Bru's dark and stormy eyes. Like a deer caught in a car's headlights, she sat frozen in this magnetic vortex, and wondered if he felt it, too.

Most likely not, she thought hazily, recovering somewhat from the unexpected hit she'd just taken to the solar plexus. No doubt he had this lazy scowl down to a practiced science. Bru's eyes gripped hers from across the room, refusing to release her, and Penelope had to grasp the arms of her chair to keep from slipping to the floor.

Good heavens. There ought to be a law against eyes like that, she thought, trembling. Sitting there mesmerized, Penelope had the eerie feeling that he could read her mind as a devilish half smirk, half smile slowly stole across his lips. His heavily fringed lashes settled at half mast, and he regarded her with a blatant look that rendered her incapable of breathing. Never had a man affected her this way before. Infuriated her. Antagonized her. Interested her.

Attracted her.

Ironically, she knew the chances that he was even aware of her as anything but a prim reminder of a past schoolmarm were slim to none. With a supreme effort, she tore her eyes from his compelling stare and focused on her hands.

It wouldn't surprise her in the least to discover that Bru was every bit as wildly popular with the ladies as his younger brother had suggested. If Mac's account of his brother's antics were any indication, he had women coming out his ears. Precisely the type of man she avoided like the plague. So why did Penelope suddenly find herself battling a ridiculous fit of melancholy that settled over her like a soupy fog? How silly. Here she was yearning for something she couldn't even put her finger on. And, all because of a little sexy eye contact with a cowboy named Conway "Bru" Brubaker.

What was she thinking? He was a client, for pity's sake. Loosening the ever-present scarf that was knotted tidily at her throat, she lifted her eyes to Buck and smiled.

"Thank you, Buck," she said as he concluded his introduction of Mac. "That was perfect." Making a small production out of checking her watch, Penelope sighed, pretending to let Bru off the introduction hook with great reluctance.

"We are running late, and I know you all have be getting on with your day, so we'll conclude this morning's introductory session. I'll tell you a little about my background in the image consulting field when we meet again this afternoon, for our last group gathering. Then…after today, we will, um…" she suddenly lost her train of thought as she dared a peek at Bru. "We will, um... um...be, uh, meeting—" she took a deep breath "—one-on-one." Averting her eyes, she grabbed her schedule book and scanned her notes. "Your, uh, father wants me to, uh...start with Conway," she said, still stammering nervously.

"Nobody calls me Conway," came the ominous growl from the other end of the table.

"Oh, yes...of course, uh, Bru." Licking her lips, she flipped through her calendar until she landed on today's date. "So, tomorrow, it will be just the two of us. Beginning with lesson one, learning to speak effectively, we will complete a six-week course that will cover such topics as, uh..."

He was staring at her. Staring at her as if she'd just lost her mind. Or stepped off a spaceship. Or forgotten to put on her blouse. And, at the moment, that was exactly how she felt under his fathomless scrutiny. Like a mindless, topless alien. Lovely.

She forged blithely ahead. "...such topics as efficient phone skills, productive social mingling, and networking made easy."

He was still staring, only now she felt as if she'd sprouted another head.

"Would you *stop?*" she snapped, slapping her calendar in exasperation and glaring pointedly at Bru.

"No problem," he drawled. "If you will recall, it wasn't my idea to start."

Regroup. Deep breath. Regroup. Ignoring him, she smiled brightly at his brothers. "After Bru graduates from his six-week training period—" *and he will if it kills me,* she thought grimly "—and with Big Daddy's approval of the...results, we will begin the second course with you, Mac. And so on, with Buck."

Mac arched a brow at Bru. The message on his face seemed clear enough. *Get rid of her, big brother.* Unfortunately, Bru's answering smirk seemed to say he was taking the challenge.

Well, Penelope thought, scowling at the arrogant grin on Bru's face, if he thought he could get rid of her that easily, he had another think coming. Wainrights always finished the job.

"So—Bru," she said, and gestured toward the handouts on the table, "please take these materials with you, and look them over. On page 3, you'll find guidelines for giving a small oral presentation. Pick any topic you like, and be prepared to speak on that subject for five minutes tomorrow morning."

She sighed. Now he was staring at her as if she'd sprouted a third eye. In each of her two heads. "In the meantime," she said, forging ahead, "I will see you all again, later this afternoon, in the library. Last night your father mentioned he'd like me to include a section on dressing successfully, so today we'll discuss the impact of color, I'll analyze each of you for your most flattering color combinations, and then we'll take some measurements in preparation for the tailor."

"*Tailor?*" Bru growled from the other end of the table.

Removing her glasses, Penelope leveled a cool, professional look in the direction of his Adam's apple. It was safer than his eyes, she figured. "Yes, your father wishes to outfit each of you with a new set of business clothes, for your reentrance into the business world. He has special plans for each of your futures within the infrastructure of Brubaker International."

Bru shook his head and ran a hand over his jaw, sagging slightly in his chair, as though he'd run out of steam. "Fine, fine, whatever." He waved an irritated hand. "What time are we supposed to be in the library this afternoon?"

She lifted her shoulders and looked curiously around the room. "Why don't you tell me what would be best for you?"

Bru snorted, and Penelope had the distinct impression that visions of hell covered in icicles were flashing behind those brooding eyes.

"Okay," she said, "how does five o'clock sound?"

Shrugging, Mac and Buck nodded. Bru was silent.

"Five it is, then," Penelope said with authority.

"Hey, Fuzzy," Bru called as he emerged from the cool, dim interior of the main stable. Squinting through the blistering Texas sunshine, he could see the grizzled ranch hand perched on a fence rail, thoughtfully chewing a toothpick. His weathered face was intent on one of the horses as it moved within the paddock.

"Hmm?" Fuzzy asked, somewhat distracted.

"You seen Buck?"

"Yeah." Fuzzy pointed to the horse he'd been watching. "Got somethin' stuck in his frog, I figure."

"Looks like," Bru said with a nod, and watched the horse as it slightly favored the hoof in question. "Where'd you see Buck?"

Jutting his chin, Fuzzy pointed toward the house with his toothpick. "Went up to the house 'bout a half-hour ago. Mac, too." Jumping off the fence, Fuzzy headed toward the limping horse.

Bru frowned. Went to the house? In the middle of the afternoon? That was strange. "What time you got?"

Fishing a gold pocket watch out of his vest, Fuzzy paused, flipped it open and peered at its face. "Half past," he called over his shoulder.

"Half past what?"

"Five."

"Aww, son of a..." Shaking his head in exasperation, Bru pushed off the fence rail and strode toward the house.

This was great. Just what he needed. Another black mark on his report card. No doubt that uppity little Miss Prim would read him the riot act about projecting an image of tardiness, and Big Daddy would be all over him like a bad smell. He sighed. Getting rid of her without incurring Big Daddy's wrath was going to take some finesse.

He grinned in spite of himself. Beating his father at his own game was never easy, but Bru loved a challenge. Sooner or later, he'd figure a way out of this mess.

Usually, he had no trouble charming the socks off any woman between the ages of nine and ninety, but then again, Penelope wasn't like any other woman he'd ever met. He'd gotten off on the wrong foot with her from the get-go. From the moment he laid eyes on her, something about Penelope Wainright had rubbed him the wrong way.

Maybe it was the fact that she made him feel like some kind of lazy hedonist, looking down her delicate little nose at him like she did. Criminy. He could have decked Mac this morning. For some reason, he hadn't wanted that Wainright woman to know about his wild party days.

They were coming to an end sooner than later, anyway. Why suffer through a bunch of lectures he didn't need? Something about her controlled manner made him feel out of control. Defensive. And more than a little ashamed of his lifestyle. He hated that feeling. Besides, he was in the process of cleaning up his act. He didn't need anybody's lessons.

She probably couldn't stand him, either.

Bru raked a hand over his face and exhaled noisily. He didn't really blame her. But dammit, anyway. It was just like the old man to pull a stunt like this, without warning. Image consultation. Sheez.

Bru sighed as he strode across the grassy approach to the long, tree-lined driveway that led to the house. It had been a dilly of a day. He wasn't much of a morning person to begin with, but being woken up by that prissy little Goldilocks, and then locked in the bathroom by his bone-head brothers, hadn't put him in the most charitable frame of mind for her little introductory session.

Bru crossed the circular drive and bounded up the front steps to the sprawling wraparound porch. Once inside the house, he followed the sound of Penelope's melodious voice across the marble entry to the library.

There, he paused in the shadows just beyond the doorway and watched her at work. Her medium-blond hair, pulled into that severe bun at the nape of her neck the way she always seemed to wear it, was the color of freshly cut hay. Wavy and silky-looking, it was kind of a golden-brown, with streaks of blonde that appeared to be the real thing. Not like the bottle blondes he liked to dance till dawn with down at The Jubilee Truckstop. And, judge of Thoroughbred horseflesh that he was, he couldn't help but notice her long, coltish legs, even under that frumpy skirt she was wearing.

Temperature rising, Bru was suddenly grateful for the cool air in the grandly marbled foyer. Tipping his hat, he wiped his forehead on his sleeve. Yep. Under that fussy business garb and that no-nonsense hairstyle there lurked a real looker. But that didn't make him like her any better. He knew a lot of beautiful women. None of them had tried to change him, turn him into something he wasn't.

Besides, Bru preferred his women—and his business dealings—a little on the wild side. Renegade that he was, Bru Brubaker did not like to follow the rules. Anybody's rules.

"...so after college, I got a job as an assistant with X-L Image in Dallas. Then, after several years, was eventually promoted to senior consultant. X-L is one of the largest firms of its kind in the country, and has an excellent success rate at turning troubled companies around."

Not wanting to interrupt, Bru removed his Stetson and settled himself against a marble column just outside the library door. He watched Penelope move slowly back and forth in front of an easel that contained a number of charts. She was still clad in the same stuffy little suit, with the same goofy little scarf, that she'd been wearing when she barged into his room that morning.

Absently Bru wondered if she slept with that silly bow

knotted at her throat. It was hard to envision her cutting loose and having any kind of fun at all. Did she ever let her hair out of that severe, businesslike style?

Nope, she was nothing like any of the women in his current social circle. As she spoke, Bru studied the graceful, fluid movements of her hands. She stepped smoothly to one side of the easel, and turned to face his brothers, and Bru had the feeling she would probably be a natural on the dance floor. Although she didn't seem like the type to enjoy a night on the town. Too bad. Years ago, his sister, Patsy, had taught him to dance, and it had come in pretty handy on more than one Saturday night.

He watched Penelope's eyes light as she spoke with animation about her career. Under those glasses of hers, she had beautiful blue eyes. He'd noticed them this morning, across the room. Deep blue, like the Texas sky where it met the horizon. They'd taken his breath away, actually. Just for a moment. And several times during the day he'd thought about those eyes. He wondered if she'd felt the same jolt he'd experienced deep in his belly when their eyes met.

Nah. Probably not. She was far too much of a prude to allow any kind of prurient interest to interfere with her perfectly planned and scheduled day.

He leaned forward slightly, his gaze traveling from her sparkling blue eyes to her lips as he tuned back into her speech.

"...a little background on what image consultation is all about. Basically, an image consultation firm, such as X-L Image, will go into a company, give a series of classes aimed at confidence-building, team-building, goal-setting and personal image consultation. After the employees have completed training, most businesses will discover anywhere from a twenty- to eighty-percent increase in their profit margins, the first year alone. This translates to dollars and cents for our clients."

Removing her glasses, Penelope ran the stem over her

lower lip as she bestowed his brothers with a relaxed smile. Bru was startled by his reaction to her simple movement. Oh, great. Now he was noticing her full, kissable-looking lips. Next thing he knew, he'd be succumbing to her image lessons and strutting around the paddock wearing some kind of prissy damn bow tie and crooking his little finger over a cup of Chef's rancid coffee.

He had to get a hold of himself. No way was Big Daddy going to get to him through a woman. Especially a woman he couldn't stand.

"I was with X-L for five years, then two years ago, for a number of personal reasons, I decided to strike out on my own as Wainright Image Consulting, and pick up the slack on a lot of the smaller jobs that X-L simply wasn't able to handle. That's how your father found out about me. Many of his companies are among some of X-L's largest clients, and they referred his current project to me. My business had grown tremendously over the last year, and this spring I hired two new consultants. They will be handling my caseload while I spend the summer working for your father."

She beamed at his brothers, then checked her wrist. Shooting an irritated glance at the door, she took a deep breath, then continued to outline her qualifications.

Bru grinned and folding his arms across his chest, made himself comfortable against the cool marble column that kept him hidden from view. He knew she was miffed by his absence, but decided to keep her waiting a while longer. Sooner or later she'd get it through her head that he was a lost cause. For now, out here in the hall, he could enjoy the view without her knowledge.

He watched her step lightly to the desk and back to face his brothers, talking all the while. Bru learned a few things about Penelope Grace Wainright. She was twenty-six years old. She lived with her wheelchair-bound mother—who was currently waiting for hip replacement surgery at the end of the summer—and a ten-year-old brother named

Randy. Her aunt was looking after the family in her absence, and her father had died right after Randy was born.

The seeds of a grudging respect were planted in the back of Bru's mind as she continued. It was obvious that she was an industrious little thing, committed to caring for her family. He had always admired strong family values and a solid work ethic, regardless of what he thought of the person.

"...probably part of the reason I took this position. My admiration for your father. You're lucky to have a caring father like Big Daddy. I envy you."

Bru rolled his eyes and snorted under his breath. Right about now, he'd like to trade Big Daddy in on a less caring model.

"Well, that about sums up my experience. I wish your brother had remembered this appointment today," Penelope said with a pained sigh as she eyed her wrist yet again. "I need to analyze your colors and get these charts filled out. I also need to make some style notations before we proceed with the tailor...."

Figuring he might as well get it over with, Bru levered himself away from the pillar and strolled into the room.

"There you are!" Penelope exclaimed. "I was beginning to think you'd forgotten."

"Forgotten?" Bru shot her his typically insolent grin as he took the empty seat behind his brothers. Pushing his hat back on his head, he asked sarcastically, "Now, how could I forget that today was color consultation day?"

Buck and Mac guffawed.

Flustered, Penelope took a step back and bumped into Big Daddy's desk. "I, uh...oh..." she stammered, and gripped the inlaid cherrywood for support. Damn the man. No one could ruffle her cool reserve like Bru Brubaker. Fighting the heat that flooded her pale complexion from head to toe, she took a deep breath and lifted her color-chip cards. "Here we are," she said, proud of the calm tone she was able to project. "We'll start by figuring out what season each of you are, then discuss some color options.''

For the next half hour, Penelope, in a flurry of activity, passed out swatches of fabric, held color charts beneath square jaws, and tried to ignore the explosion that took place in her stomach each time her gaze locked with Bru's.

Thank heaven for Mac and Buck. Their silly antics and constant joking diffused a lot of the tension. In turn, she measured each of the younger brothers and took notes on shirt size, shoe size and style preferences. And finally, when she could put it off no longer, it was Bru's turn for consultation. Buck and Mac, bored with the proceedings, and finished with their charts, asked to be excused. Reluctantly, Penelope nodded, and thanked them as they left her alone in the room with their older brother.

Clearing her throat, Penelope clutched her clipboard in her hands and, marshaling her forces of concentration, awkwardly perched on the edge of the vacant chair next to Bru. Afraid to look into his dangerous eyes, she focused on his lightly stubbled jaw and wondered where he'd gotten the small scar that graced his chin.

"I, um… Yes. We'll need your shirt size," she said to his chin. She watched, fascinated, as his lips curved into that grin she was beginning to recognize, and saw a deep dimple appear at each corner of his mouth. Classic Brubaker dimples. All three of the oldest brothers had them, but only Bru's bracketed an upper lip that seemed to curl in a permanent state of arrogant disdain. Or was it amusement? He was so hard to read.

"Where would we get that?" The dimples deepened.

Penelope swallowed. "You don't know your shirt size?"

"Should I?"

"No, I… It's just that… If you don't know, I can find out from the shirt you're wearing. I just, uh—'' she gestured to his collar ''—need to take a look at the tag.''

Bru reached for the top button of his placket. "Want

me to take it off?'' he asked. A lazy, slightly teasing quality had crept into his voice.

Was he flirting with her?

No. She knew she wasn't his type. "Oh, no,'' she hastened to assure him. "I can tell from…just turning the tag…. Uh, here, let me…'' Standing, Penelope moved around his chair and stood behind him. With tentative fingers, she pushed his incredibly soft, corn-silk hair away from his collar and fumbled for the tag. Finding it, she allowed her free hand to rest on his broad, rock-hard shoulder for support as she twisted the tag around and tried to read it. Darn, she'd left her glasses over on the desk. "Hang on, just a minute,'' she instructed and, grateful for the reprieve, dashed over to snag her glasses.

"I'm not goin' anywhere,'' he drawled, his slow gaze never leaving her legs as she moved back across the Turkish rugs that lay scattered around the highly polished wooden floor.

As she donned her glasses, Penelope also made an effort to don her professional demeanor. How unbusinesslike she was acting, allowing a client to affect her this way. She simply had to get hold of herself where Bru Brubaker was concerned. Just because he radiated a virility that would dissolve a lesser woman into a puddle of warm pudding was no reason for her to go to pieces every time their eyes made contact, for heaven's sake. Making eye contact was part of her business.

Every image consultant worth her salt knew that part of winning friends and influencing people was making—and sustaining—eye contact. It gave clients the perception that they were important, and that she was interested in them.

Heaven help her.

Filling her lungs with much-needed oxygen, Penelope turned and attempted to make professional eye contact with Bru. But the second their eyes met it was if she'd backed into an electric fence. Exhaling the breath she held in a frustrated puff, she averted her eyes from his mocking gaze and moved once again to stand behind his chair. In order to avoid physical contact as much as possible, she reached quickly back into his shirt and studied the tag.

"In case you ever need to know, you're an 18–36," she announced for his edification.

"I'll be sure to make a note of it in my diary," he answered drolly.

"Oh, uh...well, good." Tucking his tag into his shirt, she couldn't resist smoothing his hair back into place. Such soft hair on such a hard man. With an impatient shake of her head, she took her seat next to him and studied the blanks she still needed to fill on her chart.

"Shoe size?"

"Ten, I think."

"You think?"

"Want me to take 'em off?"

Was he always so willing to take everything off? Briefly she wondered what he'd do if she asked his pants size.

"No, thank you." She glanced at his booted feet. "Well, I think that will do it for today," she announced, though she was far from having all the information she needed on him. However, spending any more time in this man's presence was simply more than she had the energy for today.

"Then I'm free to go?" he asked, leaning forward and grabbing his Stetson off the floor and popping it on his head.

"Yes." Penelope could feel him looking into her eyes, but kept her face deliberately focused on her clipboard. "I'll see you first thing in the morning? Five a.m. sharp?"

Bru strode to the door, then turned and laughed. Without directly answering her question, he tipped his hat and disappeared into the hall.

Five-fifteen—a.m.

Penelope knew this, without even looking at her watch. And still no sign of Bru.

His entire family had already come, eaten, and gone on to begin their daily tasks. Mac and Buck made it down to the table, and they weren't even supposed to be here for her lesson. Swallowing the wave of fury she felt crowding into her throat, she smiled professionally at the sleepy-eyed Buck and Mac.

"Good morning."

"Mornin', Miz Wainright." Together, they nodded at her and began loading their plates at the buffet table.

"Have either of you seen Bru?"

"No, ma'am." They shook their heads and shrugged.

"Oh." Taking a deep, calming breath, Penelope slowly exhaled. "We were supposed to begin lesson one this morning. Well. Okay, then. Hmm. If you two will excuse me for a moment, I'll just go find out what's keeping him."

The two groggy brothers exchanged worried glances.

"Do you want one of us to go with you?" Buck asked. More than a little concern tinged his voice.

"Oh, no, thank you. That won't be necessary," Penelope informed him in a tightly controlled voice. "I know where his room is." Levitating on fury, she rose from her chair and, heels clicking an angry tempo, went in search of Bru.

Chapter Four

"Of all the insufferable...boorish...pigheaded...thought-less...ill-mannered...*cowboys*," Penelope spit under her breath. How he'd ever managed to pilot an entire corporation for two years with his unpredictable work ethic was beyond her. One of America's top twenty-five? Ha!

Marching furiously—which wasn't easy, considering she was wearing business pumps—across the rolling expanse of the impressive Brubaker lawn, Penelope headed around the circular drive, over the lumpy cow pasture and out to the main stable. It was there that she would most likely find Bru, she had finally been informed by one of the maids. Because, after a thorough search of his room, she'd discovered that he was no longer in bed.

Or under the bed.

Or in his closet, or even the shower, for that matter. She had, however, discovered a treasure trove of clothing and cowboy hats and boots and sundry paraphernalia under his bed and spilling out of his closet. The man really was a hedonist. But that, in her humble opinion, was the least of his problems. He'd known they had an appointment at 5:00 a.m. sharp, and he'd blown her off.

"Of all the unprofessional, inconsiderate, childish..." she continued to mutter as she reached the split-rail fence that separated the pasture from the paddock and stable areas. Pausing in her furious tracks, she pulled her reading glasses off the end of her nose and stared at the fence, pondering the best way to get to the stable. And Bru. And Bru's throat.

Hmm. No gate on this side. It was on the other side. About a mile away. Well, that was just great. Didn't matter. She was mad enough to jump the fence like a track-and-field hurdler. Only she couldn't do that. Wasn't professional.

Growling deep in her throat, Penelope stuffed her glasses into her pocket and looked around. To heck with professionalism. Hearing male voices emanating from the stable, but seeing no one, she reached down and hiked the skirt of her favorite suit up to her thighs. What was it about this place, she wondered churlishly, that always had her climbing in such an undignified manner? With an irritated shrug, she considered her options. It looked easier to go through than to go over, she decided.

Bending low, Penelope proceeded to wiggle her way through the closely spaced rails. Dirty rails. Rails that were covered with heaven only knew what. Rails that were ruining her one and only designer blouse. The white one. The one that went with everything. The one she'd paid a small fortune for. No problem, she decided, panting with exertion as she swung her long legs between the rails—she'd send the dry-cleaning bill to the incorrigible...mulish...completely deplorable...Bru.

"There," she grunted as she fell without ceremony to the ground on the other side of the fence. "Pew." Her nose wrinkled at the pungent aroma wafting from the surrounding earth. Rolling to a sitting position, she heard the snap, crackle and pop of plastic coming from somewhere beneath her fanny. She tilted her hip and felt the ground until she found the barrette that she'd used to fasten her hair back into its tidy bun that morning. No biggie, she thought, and stuffed the broken barrette into her pocket, along with her precious reading glasses. She had another one.

Shoving her hair out of her eyes, she grasped the middle rail and, huffing and puffing, pulled herself upright. Unfortunately, her scarf had other ideas, and Penelope suddenly found herself jerked to her knees, and tethered to the fence by her bow tie. *Owwchhh!* Pain ricocheted from her knees to her ankles and back to her knees again. Her stockings were officially garbage.

"Ishhhh," she ground out between her tightly clenched jaws. "Of all the stupid...*blasted...annoying...irksome...*" She spit each word with a vehemence that would have fired bullets from a gun without a trigger as she wrestled the ends of her scarf away from the long splinters that held her captive. "Oh, for the love of..." Finally frustrated beyond endurance, she managed to unfold her battered legs and achieve a semiupright position. Then she grabbed hold of her scarf and, with a mighty yank, tore the fabric free, nearly sending herself over backward in the process. Gaining her balance, she squared her shoulders and took a deep, calming breath.

Relax. Regroup. Relax, she chanted to herself, struggling to regain some semblance of professionalism. With a toss of her head—she couldn't stand the way her hair fell in her face without a barrette—she quickly surveyed the damage, and dusted off her backside. Pulling off her ruined panty hose, Penelope stuffed them in her pocket, along with her barrette and glasses. That accomplished, she shoved her skirt back down to where it was supposed to be and slid her feet back into her pumps.

And, as she did so, the tiny hairs at the back of her neck began to tingle. The voices in the stable had stopped talking. Someone was watching her, she just knew it. Summoning as much dignity as she could muster, given the situation, she slowly turned around and leveled her mortified gaze at the leering pack of ranch hands who stood leaning against an old wooden wagon, their lecherous grins splitting their weathered faces from ear to ear.

And the insufferable Bru, his Brubaker dimples in full bloom, was leading the pack.

Swallowing the wave of fury that turned her cheeks a brilliant shade of crimson, Penelope gathered her wits and what was left of her scarf and tiptoed stoically across the manure-sprinkled paddock toward the gathering of men. What choice did she have, after all? As much as she wanted to turn tail and run, she couldn't. Wainrights never retreated, no matter how formidable the foe.

"Hello," she chirped brightly, hoping to belie the sparks that she knew were literally shooting from her eyes. *Win friends,* she reminded herself. *Influence people.* She nodded pleasantly at the half-dozen grinning jerks in cowboy hats. Hadn't they ever seen a businesswoman before? she wondered churlishly. "Could I speak to you a moment?" Penelope asked in a tightly controlled voice as she came to a stop in front of Bru. She knew she had murder in her eyes, but she was too livid to worry about her image at the moment.

"Uh-oh, boss. Looks like you're in trouble with the teach," a scruffily bearded ranch hand said. Raucous laughter echoed off the side of the massive stable.

"Eeyep," drawled another red-faced hand, "I'd be countin' my fingers when she's done with you, Bru old buddy." More rowdy howling from the cowboy faction.

"I don't know," a sour-looking hand with a scar on his cheek said. "Mebbe she's the one needs to be taught."

Arching a faintly amused brow, Bru waved off his staff. "You clowns shut up and get back to work." Amid a wave of disappointed moans and groans, the hands—grinning idiotically all the while—shuffled off to do as they were told.

"What can I do for you?" Bru asked in an offhand manner as he turned and headed toward the stable.

Penelope stood there, mouth agape, and stared at his retreating form. "What can you *do* for me?" She hobbled after him, her knees protesting in agony. *"What can you do for me?"* she shrieked, in a most unprofessional manner, and shoved her hair out of her face.

Pausing in the stable's yawning doorway, Bru turned and looked over his shoulder at her. A strange expression crossed his face for a moment as he allowed his gaze to rove over her hair, her soiled blouse and finally her battle-scarred shins. It was an expression that Penelope thought she recognized from yesterday morning, when their eyes had locked for the first time. With a sharp shake of his head, it was gone.

"You're here, aren't you? I figure you must want something."

"Are you daft?" she shouted, and continued after him, gingerly picking her way between the fresher horse patties in her scuffed and soiled pumps. She was going to have to burn her shoes.

"Daft?"

"We had an appointment this morning."

"Correction. *You* had an appointment this morning." Without waiting for her, he ambled down the stable's broad hallway and headed toward the tack room.

Following him through the giant double doors that led into the huge building, Penelope blinked, letting her eyes adjust to the sudden dimness of the stable. Dust floated slowly in the slanting rays of sunshine that filtered through cracks in the stable's walls, illuminating the stalls and their curious occupants. Soft nickers and whinnies welcomed Penelope, beckoning her to come rub a velvety nose. She took a deep breath, and the smell of horse and hay and leather filled her senses. Oh, what a wonderful place, she thought reverently, understanding a little better now why Bru was so compelled to work here. Just standing in this building, soaking up the environment, filled her with excitement. She wondered what it would be like to ride one of these horses. Thrilling, she was sure.

However, a passion for his chosen work did not excuse him from standing her up for this morning's appointment. She'd been hired to do a job, and by gum she would do it. Moving down the wide walkway between the stalls, Penelope nearly collided with Bru as he emerged from the tack room carrying a saddle and bridle. With a curt nod of acknowledgment, he moved around her and disappeared into a stall labeled Lightning.

"Would you please stand still for a moment?" Penelope groused in exasperation as she joined him in the stall with a beautiful animal that she guessed must be Lightning. Unable to help herself, she smiled and reaching up stroked his smooth, pliant nose.

Nudging Penelope aside, Bru slipped a halter over Lightning's head. Expertly fastening it into place, he turned the horse around and lead him outside the stall, where he tied him to a post. "Keep talkin'. I can hear ya," he mumbled from somewhere out in the hallway, on the other side of Lightning's barrel belly.

The horse's broad behind filled the stall's doorway. Bobbing up and down on tiptoe, Penelope tried to catch a glimpse of Bru as she spoke. He'd done it on purpose, blocking her this way. Coward.

"I...uh..." With a tail swishing mildly in her face, Penelope felt as if she were talking to the horse's rump. Patting his flank, she squeezed between the stall and the horse and moved to the post where Lightning was tied, in order to get a better view of Bru. "Would you mind telling me why you stood me up again this morning?" Penelope demanded, watching in fascination as Bru went through the motions of grooming and saddling Lightning.

"Didn't feel like it."

"Didn't feel like it? Didn't *feel* like it?" Poking her head beneath the rope that tethered the horse, she stared at Bru. "What kind of an answer is that?" Lightning nuzzled her neck, snorting into her hair, tugging the strands with his lips, and it was all she could do to suppress a grin of delight.

Bru shrugged. "I don't need image lessons."

"Aha!" A disbelieving squeak of laughter escaped her slack lips as she tugged a lock of hair out of Lightning's mouth. Must be time to condition her hair, if the horse was confusing it for straw. "Excuse me? Well, according to your father, you do. And if your behavior this morning is any indication of how you ran the show down at Brubaker International, I can just bet that you—"

A loud crack brought Penelope up short as Bru fired a currycomb into the stall, where it bounced off the wall and clattered to the floor by the doorway. The horse must have been used to his fits of temper, because the animal barely flinched.

"According to my father, I need a lot of things," he said, his voice deadly calm as he returned her stare, "that I'm managing to do just fine without."

Two nosy ranch hands wandered down the expansive corridor between the stalls. It was clear from their shuffling gate and whispered words that they were trying to figure out what was going on between the boss and his uppity little image teacher. A gaggle of Curious Georges who had gathered back in the entryway, drinking coffee and cracking ribald jokes were waiting for a report. Obviously, Bru had filled them in on the reasons for her presence at the ranch this summer, and it would seem that they all found it as entertaining as he did.

"Fuzzy?" Bru called from around the horse.

Penelope glanced at the two men who froze in their tracks. They looked like kids who'd been caught stealing.

"Uh...yeah?" Fuzzy asked.

"What are you guys doin'?"

"Oh, well, me and Red here, we was, uh…just, uh…lookin' for…" Fuzzy looked at the ruddy-complexioned man at his side. "What was we lookin' for?"

Red reddened and glanced to the floor of Lightning's stall. "Why, uh, we was lookin' for the currycomb."

"Tack room has a bucketful," Bru said, and tossed a saddle blanket over Lightning's back.

"Well, now, that's true," Fuzzy agreed, "but we was lookin' for the good currycomb."

"The special one," Red put in.

"Get out of here," Bru said, and grinned at Penelope. The two men made an abrupt about-face and shuffled back to the faction loitering by the door. Relaxing against the wall of the stall, Bru tucked a piece of straw in the corner of his mouth and watched them go.

Penelope's eyes strayed to the corner of his mouth, where the straw bobbed as he slowly chewed it. She swallowed. Something about his lazy stance did strange things to her insides. Her gaze traveled north, and once again their eyes tangled, with a jolt that would have put a power line to shame. What was it about Bru Brubaker that had her insides suddenly squirrelier than a roller-coaster ride?

"They don't get to see many pretty women out here in the stables. You're kind of a novelty."

Ducking back to the other side of the horse, Penelope waited for the warmth in her cheeks to dissipate. He thought she was pretty? Her? She blinked and swallowed. "Flattery will get you nowhere," she groused, feeling inordinately pleased at his words.

"That doesn't surprise me," he admitted as he hoisted the saddle onto Lightning's back.

With a step backward, Penelope watched in fascination as he proceeded to fasten a number of buckles and straps. Nudging the horse's belly with his knee, he spoke gently to the animal and tightened the cinch. Then he slipped the bridle into the horse's mouth and, fastening another series of buckles, removed the halter and gathered the reins in his hand.

A soft clicking sound from Bru had the giant animal following him as docilely as a lamb.

Nonplussed, Penelope watched him walk away without so much as a by-your-leave.

Was that it? The extent of his excuse for not taking lesson one—learning to speak effectively? "I didn't *feel* like it?" He could simply tell her he didn't feel like it, and walk away as if nothing were wrong? Once again, Penelope felt her pulse pick up speed.

Well, buster, she fumed, marching after him, there were a lot of things she didn't particularly feel like doing, either. Coaching him on his image being number one on the hit parade. But she did them nevertheless. Because she was a professional. Because she was a Wainright. Because...she needed the money.

"Missster Brubaker," she called imperiously to the impenetrable wall of his back.

"Yep, keep talkin'," he shot over his shoulder. "I can hear ya."

"You still have not answered my question." She rushed as fast as her pumps would allow, to keep up with his lanky, fluid stride.

"Um-humm." Bru continued to lead Lightning into the morning sunshine. Then, pausing by the hay wagon, he grabbed the saddle horn and hoisted himself onto the horse's back as easily as if he'd been born there.

Hands on hips, she stood looking up at him, feeling no end to her exasperation. How was she supposed to do her job, when her client kept running away? she wondered, her chin trembling. How was she supposed to please Big Daddy enough to earn her bonus? The bonus that would pay for her mother's surgery? For Randy's school books? How was she supposed to corral the elusive Bru Brubaker long enough to teach him *anything?* Rapidly she blinked back tears of frustration, refusing to cry in front of him. It simply wasn't professional. Wainrights never cried in public.

With a gentle sound and a nudge of his boot, Bru guided Lightning the few steps to Penelope, and extended his hand to her. "Come on," he said around the piece of straw that still dangled in the corner of his permanently smirking lips.

"What?"

"Give me your hand."

"Why?" she demanded, wondering what he was up to now.

"Let's go."

"Where?"

"You always so full of questions?"

"Yes."

"Who cares where?" he growled, reaching down and grasping her hand.

Before she knew what hit her, Penelope found herself sitting sidesaddle in the circle of Bru's arms, firmly wedged somewhere between the saddle horn and...him.

"But what about lesson one? Learning to speak effectively?" she babbled aloud, dazedly rambling on as she looked around from her lofty perch.

"Who gives a rat's backside?"

His hands around her waist, Bru tugged on the reins and urged Lightning out of the paddock, to the road that stretched over the horizon, where the crystal-clear blue of the Texas sky met the golden waves of an endless sea of grass. Lightning did not need to be told twice. Hitting the open road, the animal moved from the jarring jog to a smooth, undulating canter that had Penelope's heart singing with wild joy.

Oh my goodness. Oh, my goodness! Oh! My! Goodness! They were flying!

Unable to help herself, Penelope, who was now grinning and literally bubbling over with delight, leaned back against the hard wall of Bru's chest. Even though she'd never been on a horse before in her life, she wasn't afraid.

Bru wouldn't let her fall, she knew, completely secure in his strength and his skill.

Gracious, she thought, looking around. It was so high up here on top of a horse! She'd never known how on top of the world one felt when horseback riding. No wonder Bru didn't want to go back to the stuffy old smoke-filled boardroom of Brubaker International. Who in their right mind would ever want to imprison themselves in such a manner when they could be out here...*flying!*

For what seemed like miles they traveled, gliding down the road, which appeared to lead to nowhere in particular. Penelope, having finally settled into the rhythm of the horse's movement, began to enjoy the scenery. The endless acreage that made up Big Daddy's range was breathtaking. One rolling golden hill after another melted into the horizon as they left civilization, and Penelope couldn't be sure if the pitter-patter of her heartbeat was caused by the view, or the muscular arms that held her against the masculine body, rock-solid from life on the ranch.

The combination of sensations was exhilarating. Never before had she experienced anything so completely and gloriously overwhelming. And, as much as she hated to admit it, she was beginning to realize it had much more to do with the man who cradled her body than with the impromptu ride.

What was Bru thinking? she wondered. Riding must be second nature to him. Old hat. And holding a woman in his arms this way was most likely more of the same. Taking the teacher for a ride was probably just another mundane task in his busy day. Although, if he minded taking the time to show her around the ranch, his impatience did not show. He urged Lightning on, over hill and dale, as though he had all the time in the world.

No longer bound by her usual barrette, Penelope's loose hair was whipped wildly by the wind across her cheeks, behind her shoulders and into her eyes. Pushing it back, away from her face, she turned slightly and, lifting her head from beneath his chin, chanced a peek up at Bru. Slowly he angled his face and grinned down at her, with the familiar devastating impishness that curled his upper lip and cut deep crevasses into the corners of his mouth. His curving lips hovered a whisper away from her own. What would his kiss be like? she wondered, knowing that if his eyes could melt her from across the room, his lips would most likely set them on fire.

Good heavens! Where were these unprofessional thoughts coming from? He was a client, for pity's sake. She had never, in all her years as a successful image consultant, ever had to fight the urge to kiss a client. Unbidden, curiosity burned twin spots of color high on her cheeks as she jerked her head back away from the danger zone of his lips. The quickening of her pulse brought the stirring of something new deep inside. An ache. A yearning. A need for something that she hadn't known until this very moment was missing from her life.

Penelope's breath caught in her throat as Bru's dark eyes sought hers and, tangling with them, held them for a powerful moment before they strayed off toward the horizon. Tightening his grip ever so slightly around her waist, he pulled her back against his body, and settled his square jaw at the side of her head. His hands were work-roughened and lean, and she studied them where they lay cradled in her lap, holding the leather reins against her thigh.

Settling back, she let her eyes travel to the point where their thighs met, hers covered in her soft summer-weight wool skirt, and his corded with muscles and encased in pliant, well-worn denim. Denim that was soft as a baby's cheek. She could feel it beneath her bare legs. The work shirt he wore was soft and comfortable, as well, and, unable to control herself, she burrowed against the steady rise and fall of his chest. Again she felt his arms pull her slightly closer, and her heart picked up speed.

This entire experience was so alien to her. The complete

and total antithesis of the self-restraint she attempted at all times to exude. Aware that she was succumbing to the call of the wild, but suddenly not caring, she gave in to the giddy feeling of excitement that welled into—and burned against—the back of her throat. She could teach him to speak effectively another time, she decided, throwing caution to the wind. For now, she would concentrate on getting to know what made Bru tick. Knowing one's enemy was helpful in conquering. Whatever made this man tick, it brought out a side of her personality that she hadn't known existed. Yes, like it or not, Bru unleashed something in her that she couldn't seem to control.

With ease, Lightning came to the crest of a hill, barely laboring under the added weight of his extra passenger. The sun was already rising, lifting away from its golden seat on the eastern horizon, and casting its warm rays across the Brubaker land. Pulling the horse to a stop beneath a shade tree, Bru gestured toward the other side of the knoll.

"That silver ribbon down there in the gully," Bru murmured, his voice rumbling low into her ear as he gestured toward a point way off in the distance, "running through the stand of trees, is an irrigation stream. Over there, off to the side, is a man-made pond for the cattle. We call 'em tanks. Used to swim in 'em, when we were kids. Still do, sometimes."

Penelope smiled, envisioning the lively Brubaker brood cooling off on a hot summer day. Her brother, Randy, would love to have so much open space to run in. Not trusting herself to look up at Bru, she kept her eyes directed straight ahead and pointed off to the west. "What's beyond that?" she wondered aloud.

A chuckle resonated in his chest. "For about as far as the eye can see, about ten thousand acres of prime ranch land. Cattle and grazing pasture, mostly. Some hay and grain fields in the back sections. Those rocking horses you see over there in the west section are oil pump jacks. Folks call 'em rocking horses, 'cause if you stare at 'em they kind of look like grazing horses. They pump the oil out of the ground.'' Leaning impossibly closer, he pointed to the areas of which he was speaking. "But most of Big Daddy's oil fields are off campus, so to speak.''

Penelope could feel him grin against the side of her head. His jaw rasped pleasantly in her hair and, reaching up, he tugged some strands over her shoulder. Then, for reasons her thrumming heart couldn't begin to fathom, he left his hand on her shoulder, his fingertips lightly brushing her nape.

"Oh," she breathed, her throat tightening in an effort to keep her stomach from leaping past her laboring lungs. His nearness was making intelligent conversation impossible. "Where, uh, where does this road go?" she squeaked, wondering why her usual methods of speaking effectively were failing her now.

"All the way around the perimeter of the property that way. This way—" he pointed in a different direction "—leads to the pump jacks, so the oil trucks can get in and empty the oil tanks.'' His hand slid from the nape of her neck, and traveled slowly down her arm to the back of her hand, where it rested lightly. He tilted his head, and Penelope could tell that he was looking at her for a moment.

She gave in to the urge to look back at him. "Oh." Not for a million dollars could she have thought of another thing to say. "Ohhhh," she repeated stupidly and nodded. There was a lot more to ranch life than met the eye. She was impressed.

"'Bout a days ride to the west, in what we call the west cabin section, there's a cabin that the ranch hands use when they're out mending fences and counting head in the holding pens...." Lines crinkled at the corners of his eyes. "Other than that, just a lot of fence posts and more rocking horses and about fifteen different sections of ranch land.''

"Oh." Surely she could think of something else to say,

something more effective than "Oh." Her heart pounded as he rested his chin against her temple.

"Well, I should probably be gettin' you back."

No! she wanted to shout. *Not yet.* She wanted to see the cabin and the cattle and the pasture and the oil fields. She even wanted to see the rest of the fence posts, if it meant spending more time riding on the wind. More time getting to know Bru. More time pressed against his body and wrapped in his arms.

"Y-yes," she stammered, a dollop of melancholy splashing into her stomach. Sighing, she felt like a petulant child. "Yes. I should probably be getting back." Although what she'd be getting back to was a good question. Her student, not to mention all the fun, was out here on the range.

"You probably have a lot to do," Bru said conversationally. Tugging on the reins, he nudged Lightning with his foot and headed back the way they'd come, toward the house.

Penelope shot him a scathing look.

Letting his head tilt back, Bru's laughter flowed. "Nothing to do?" He laughed again. "Poor baby. I guess you'll just have to hand in your resignation. That, or lay by the pool and collect your pay."

"I'll *earn* my pay, thank you very much," she snapped. "Starting this afternoon. What time will you be home?" Instead of looking up at him, she rested her head against the hollow of his throat and lifted her chin. She loved the way his voice rumbled, deep in his chest.

"Umm..." Bru thought for a moment. "I don't know. Afternoon, sometime, I guess."

"By four?" she prodded.

"Well, I need to make a few phone calls. Then I need to head to town for a cattle auction to check on market prices. After that, I have to head over to see the vet and talk to him about some more blackleg vaccine and fly spray. And then—" a smile stole into his voice "—I have to see a man about a horse."

Leaning back, Penelope arched a brow up at him.

He laughed. "Really."

"By four-thirty?" she pressed.

He shook his head and grinned. "Probably."

"Okay. Meet me in the library at five. We can go over some of the materials I know that you've read."

Bru snorted.

The miles that carried them home disappeared far too quickly for Penelope's taste. However, she knew that she hadn't been hired to spend her days disrupting ranch business and riding horses and developing a crush on her employer's rebellious son. She cringed, astonished at herself for even thinking of a client in such a manner. Giving her head an impatient shake, she willed herself to stop being such a ninny, and start acting like the professional she was.

Before she knew it, the stables were looming ahead.

Bru guided Lightning around the main stable, over the pasture and, to Penelope's surprise, down the circular drive and across the sprawling lawn. Reining the horse to a stop near the palatial entryway to the main house, Bru gripped Penelope around the waist and helped her slide off the horse and onto the steps. Breathless, she grabbed the railing for support and looked up at him.

He leaned forward in a conspiratorial manner that had her heart skipping beats again. Was he going to kiss her? she wondered excitedly. No, she realized, her cheeks reddening at her ludicrous thoughts.

"Don't tell my mother I've been riding on the lawn," he whispered with a grin. "She never has liked that."

"I won't, if you promise to show up at five," she retorted, returning his grin.

"Hey, boss." It was Fuzzy, standing in the driveway, his hands planted on his hips. "Where you been?"

Behind Fuzzy, the ranch hand with the scar across his

cheek stood, making no attempt to hide his interest in Penelope's bare legs.

"Riding." Bru never took his eyes off Penelope.

Flustered, Penelope groped for something to say in front of the curious ranch hands. Something professional. Something that would lend credibility to the fact that she'd just spent the morning, out on the range, alone with the boss.

"Remember to be back by five," she said. "Today, we will cover several easy steps to making a good first impression." She figured Bru needed this session more than he needed speaking effectively. And if she was only going to get a minute of his time, here and there, she wanted to hit the highlights.

"A good first impression." He rolled his eyes.

"Yes," she said with a glance at Fuzzy. The old geezer was laughing. "My simple formula will work wonders for you, and will have business associates eating out of your hand."

Bru tucked his chin into his shoulder and looked back at Fuzzy. "Hear that, Fuzzy?"

"I ain't eatin' outa your hand," the old man groused good-naturedly, and ambled off down the drive. "Come on, Jim," he called to the hand with the scarred cheek. "We got work to do."

"Work, work, work," Jim grumbled and, with a last wolfish appraisal of Penelope's legs, shuffled off after Fuzzy.

Penelope pursed her lips. Someday, they would take her seriously. Someday, they would see the importance of image. She sighed. Someday, when pigs taxied down the circular drive for takeoff. Mustering her dignity, she turned and climbed the stairs. "Five," she called over her shoulder, hoping—and not for the most professional of reasons—that Bru would not forget. She paused at the top of the steps and looked over her shoulder, but Bru was already gone.

* * *

Tired and aching from a long, hot, tedious day, Bru pulled his truck into its usual spot at the end of the circular drive near the main house and turned off the engine. He glanced at his watch and shrugged. After six. No doubt Penelope would be steamed. Good.

For the hundredth time since he'd deposited her on the front steps, he wondered what she'd done all day long. He'd experienced random urges to return home, clean up and make it to class on time, but he'd managed to resist those flirtations with insanity. He dragged a hand over his jaw. What was it about little Miss Prim that got under his skin that way? Made him want to cooperate with this ridiculous image charade, just to spare her feelings?

He groaned at the memory of her standing by the split-rail fence, eyes and hair wild, her scarf in tatters, her stockings shredded as she wiggled her way out of them and shoved them into her pocket. Her legs were the stuff fantasies were made of, and he had had to endure more than one observation by the ranch hands as to the shapely turn of her ankles. Her calves. Her knees. Her…thighs.

"Reminiscent of Barbarella, the way she fought her way through the split rails," Fuzzy had said, his eyes slightly glassy at the image. Red had disagreed. "More like Sheena, queen of the paddock," he'd thought, his usually ruddy complexion growing ruddier. Yeah, they'd all nodded in agreement. She was somethin', all right. They'd nearly driven him crazy with questions about their little ride earlier that morning.

He still couldn't have said what had possessed him to grab her and haul her up onto Lightning's back for an impromptu tour of the ranch. Talk about fraternizing with the enemy. The smell of her perfume still clung to his shirt.

Frustrated, Bru pounded the steering wheel.

She had to quit.

If he was going to win this round with Big Daddy, that had to be the plan. As long as he didn't get sidetracked by a pair of shapely legs, he'd be all right. Bru didn't want to like her. He didn't want to wonder about her. To want her. She was part of Big Daddy's agenda, and in that light, he wanted nothing to do with her, whatsoever. Then why, he wondered as he unfastened his seat belt—a *seat belt* for crying in the night—was he going to go look for her now? What kind of a spell had she cast on him? He was walking into Big Daddy's trap like a lamb to the slaughter. He had to fight it. Yes. Fight.

He would go look for her to tell her to forget any lessons with him. She should start with Mac. Or Buck. Or, shucks, even Fuzzy, if she wanted to. Just leave him alone.

"Grrrr..." he growled, climbing out of his shiny red four-wheel-drive rig and slamming the door. He was losing his mind.

Following the sounds of laughter and splashing that drifted out to the driveway from behind the house, Bru ambled out to the pool. Several of his brothers ran around the edge of the pool, shoving, diving, yelling, splashing and generally showing off for the benefit of Penelope, who sat in a lounge chair, giggling and encouraging them. Moving closer, but staying hidden behind the shrubbery that grew next to the pool house, he watched the goings-on for a while, before his eyes finally landed on Penelope.

What the heck kind of a getup was that? he mused, taking in the little ruffly skirt that skimmed the bottom of her chaste one-piece swimming suit. And why the heck did he find it such a turn-on? After all, it wasn't as if anything but her arms and legs were exposed to the sunlight. Just her arms and those incredibly long, shapely legs.

"Hey, Penelope! Watch!" Hank, Bru's youngest brother, shouted, before cannonballing into the deep end.

Bru shook his head. She'd even managed to get to his eleven-year-old brother, he noted, watching Hank surface and turn to her, waiting for her approval.

"Wow, Hank," Penelope praised. "That was the biggest splash of the day."

Hank grinned and paddled over toward her. Meanwhile,

Johnny and Willie vied for her attention on the diving board. "Watch this, Penelope," Johnny called and, picking his brother up, threw him over his shoulder, where he landed on Waylon. Letting out a war whoop, Waylon grabbed Johnny's ankle and dragged him kicking and screaming off the diving board and into the water. Strangely, Bru felt an irrational stab of jealousy zing through his gut. These chowderheads had had the pleasure of spending the day with her, while he was out busting his butt for a living. They were all pretty chummy with her, too, he noted sourly, as he watched Mac and Johnny hoist themselves out of the water and threaten to toss Penelope into the drink. He'd never be rid of Wainright Image Consulting if his brothers kept palavering with her and showing her a good time. She was supposed to be sitting here fuming.

She squealed in protest as they picked her up and carried her to the deep end.

"Just get it over with!" she cried, giggling and kicking her feet and waving her arms. Gleefully, they pitched her overboard, and then jumped in after her, cavorting and howling like a bunch of lustful lunatics after a ruffly-skirted mermaid.

"Boys!" Miss Clarise called from the second story veranda. "Time to get out of the pool. Chef tells me that supper will be served buffet-style in a half hour on the back patio. Please, go get dressed now."

Amazingly, Bru's brothers did as they were bidden without much fuss, and disappeared into the pool house. Yes, she had definitely cast some sort of magical spell over them all, Bru decided, watching with his jaw slightly slack.

Lazily paddling to the edge of the pool, Penelope climbed up the ladder. Moving over to her lounge chair, she began to gather her belongings, stuffing magazines and suntan lotion into a large, goofy-looking wicker-type purse.

Angling her head, Miss Clarise smiled down at their

guest. "I hope you like tacos, Penelope. The boys put their request in this morning."

"Sounds wonderful," Penelope said with a smile. "I'll be along shortly."

"Take your time, darling," Bru's mother drawled in her soft, cultured Southern voice. She smiled. "Despite their best intentions, the boys are always a bit tardy. 'Specially Bru." Miss Clarise smiled sympathetically, then disappeared into the house.

Penelope was alone.

His palms suddenly as clammy as a schoolboy's, Bru moved out from behind the foliage growing up against the pool house and stepped through the intricate iron gate that swung between the sections of brick fencing. He could hear his brothers laughing and clowning around inside the pool house. He tuned them out. He had to stay focused.

"There you are!" Penelope cried, spying him as he came into the pool yard. Lowering her sunglasses, she narrowed her eyes at him. "This is the third time you've stood me up." She seemed too relaxed at the moment to muster much anger.

"Sorry."

"Are you?"

Suddenly he was. Very sorry. He'd love to have spent the afternoon in her company. But, he reminded himself, that was neither here nor there. She was just more of Big Daddy's brand of interference in his life. Interference he could live without.

He shrugged. "Couldn't be helped."

"Okay." She sighed, standing there, so guileless in that little ruffly suit that was far more alluring than any bikini he'd ever laid eyes on. "I've been thinking."

"Yeah, me too," he said, wondering how he should inform her that he wouldn't be taking any of her image classes. For some reason, she seemed to have her heart set on cleaning up his act.

Pulling her sunglasses off, she chewed the stem. "Since

you are obviously not a morning person—" she studied him thoughtfully "—and you don't exactly seem to be an afternoon person, I thought we should try again tomorrow, in the evening. You've already missed Tuesday's and to-day's classes. If you start tomorrow—" she glanced at her watch "—which is…Thursday evening, I can bring you up to speed just in time for the ICAA party this Saturday night." She beamed, obviously having spent some time working these logistics out.

"The what?" Bru frowned. Party? No thanks. He was trying to cut down. "What's a CIA party?"

A tiny smile tugged at her lips. "The ICAA. Our state chapter of The Image Consultants of America Association has a party once a month so that our clients can practice the social skills they've been learning in a controlled sit-uation. They stagger the parties across the state, and this month the party's being held in Dallas, which is lucky for us."

"Oh." *Ugghh*. He was going to throttle Big Daddy.

"I'll tell you about it tomorrow evening during class. Then, Friday night, we'll review—then, Saturday, the party."

She looked so earnest standing there, her large, liquid baby blues staring up at him. He battled the urge to grab her and shock her flip-flops off with a kiss so hot the pool would boil.

"Don't look so worried," she said with a laugh. "The ICAA party is part of the course. Your brothers will have to go to one during their individual sessions, as well." Reaching down, she snagged her silly wicker pool bag. "Your mother wants me to go get ready for supper. Tacos." Penelope smiled. "So," she said as she turned to go, "our first session will begin tomorrow evening at eight. We will have to study hard to make up for lost time. Oh—" she paused "—don't worry about what to wear to the ICAA party Saturday night. Your mother found your tuxedo in the storage closet and sent it out to be dry-cleaned. So, you're all set."

Bru watched her toss him an airy wave, then sway fetchingly out of the pool yard.

"Eight o'clock sharp tomorrow night," she called. "I'll remind you again at dinner, and then again tomorrow at breakfast." There was a teasing note in her voice.

He scratched his head and sighed. She expected him to wear a tuxedo to a business party this Saturday night? Aww, man. His fingers strayed to the back of his neck, and he began to rub the knotted muscles there. He had to give Big Daddy points for digging up the determined, professional Penelope. She was as perky as a wirehaired terrier, and twice as tenacious. His grudging respect for her spunk was growing. Especially given the fact that he'd gone out of his way to be so uncooperative.

Oh, well... Bru figured there would be time enough tomorrow night at eight to tell her that she would just have to take one of his brothers to this shindig of hers. He was too tired to deal with it at the moment. She would simply have to get it through her head that he was not going to take her image lessons. No matter how badly he might need them.

Right now, he was going to take a shower and have a sandwich in his room. Because it would seem that the more time he spent in Penelope's company, the more he liked her. And if there was one thing Bru didn't want, it was to like Penelope Wainright.

Chapter Five

Penelope was really beginning to dislike Bru in earnest.

The following evening found her waiting for him yet again, as she rocked to and fro on a lower porch swing near the house's magnificent entrance. Jaw clenched tightly shut, back ramrod-straight, she stared into the distance and rocked. And rocked. Every so often, lips twitching in irritation, she would shift her gaze from the lamplit scenery and zero in on her watch.

He was standing her up. Again.

For almost two hours now, she'd been waiting, rocking, and hoping against hope that he'd be a gentleman and show up. But, alas, as she had already surmised, Bru was no gentleman. The air-conditioned house beckoned, but she ignored the temptation, preferring instead to sit in the humidity and wait for an opportunity to give the eldest Brubaker son a piece of her mind.

Agitated, she jumped to her feet and began to pace in an effort to quell the panic that was beginning to crowd into her throat. The ICAA party was looming ahead day after tomorrow, and they hadn't even started the necessary courses yet. The party was extremely important to her professionally. It gave her and other area consultants a chance to network, while at the same time allowing the students to try their image wings. The heels of her pumps clicked against the wooden floor as she strode back and forth between the white siding of the house and the ornate railing that circled the porch. *What if he stood her up for the party?* she wondered, a fresh surge of anxiety knotting her stomach.

Then again, *What if he didn't?* With no image lessons under his belt, what would her contemporaries think of her abilities as a consultant when she arrived at the party with the irreverent Bru? Unfortunately, in order for a student to graduate from one of her courses, the student in question was required to attend an ICAA party. She could not—and would not—change her course rules just to accommodate Bru. Especially since he'd been so unaccommodating himself.

Generally she encouraged all of her clients to invite their significant others to the party to join in the festivities. However, Bru was a different story. Good gracious, who would he get it into his head to invite as his guest? The idea of Bru bringing along one of his...his "friends" was unsettling for a myriad of reasons that she dared not explore.

Ohhh. She pushed her fingertips into her throbbing temples and moaned. Surely, even if she managed to survive this debacle, she would never work in this town again, once people discovered that she'd been the one to teach the renegade Bru how to conduct himself in public. Some birds squawked from the branch of a distant mesquite tree, echoing her desire to scream.

She was going to kill him.

Penelope was a doer. She made lists and stuck to them. For as long as she could remember, every evening without fail, she had planned the following day in her business diary. She would even go so far as to write "Get out of bed'' in the first slot just so that she could enjoy the satisfaction of crossing it off and forging on to complete the next task. Rarely did she ever allow herself to deviate from her course of action. No surprises for Penelope. Her days were regimented. Planned. Organized. Structured.

Although, for all the good it was doing her with that boorish Bru, she might as well throw her diary out the window. The birds squawked again.

"Oh, shut up," she muttered, finally deciding she might as well go in. Bru was evidently in town for the duration, kicking up his heels at the local watering hole. Probably had dance partners lined up clear out to the front doors, too. Blinking rapidly, Penelope bit her lip against a sudden fit of melancholy and, with a heavy sigh, gathered up her class materials from where she'd left them on the swing.

She was failing. And Wainrights never failed.

As she listlessly unsnapped the clasp to her briefcase, a familiar roar echoed down the driveway. She lifted her chin, and her heart skipped a beat as she spied the approaching red tornado. Bru. Finally. Slowly straightening, she watched his arrival, attempting to muster some of her flagging indignation. Unfortunately, the fact that she was so incredibly relieved to see him negated most of her ire.

After he screeched to his customary stop, the truck door swung open and, in his typically leggy fashion, Bru disembarked and ambled across the driveway. Spotting her standing on the porch near the front door, he hesitated for a moment. Probably afraid she'd be all over him like a bad case of the hives, she mused, forcing a power smile at his brooding face. She would not let him get the best of her. Oh, no.

Bru glanced around. Then, seeming to figure he had no choice, he strode across the lawn and bounded up the front porch steps.

"You're late." She was proud of her neutral, professional tone. If truth be told, she wanted to jump up and down and lunge at him.

He shrugged. "Couldn't be helped."

Obviously, he did not feel obligated to elaborate. "Ever hear of a phone?"

Jutting his chin defiantly, he angled a piercing look straight into her eyes. "Look, Penny," he growled, his expression dark, ominous.

"Nobody calls me Penny," she snapped.

A muscle jumped in his jaw, and Penelope couldn't tell if he was going to laugh or turn her over his knee. "Miz Wainright—"

"Penelope will suffice," she said coolly, interrupting him.

"Whatever." Rolling his eyes, he moved up to the top step and grasped one of the imposing Greek-style columns that supported the entrance to the porch. He leaned against the column and dragged a tired hand through his hair. "Look, Penelope, can the lecture wait? I've had a long day, and I'm starving."

"No!" she cried, and smacked the course materials she'd been loading into her briefcase on the railing for emphasis. His eyes widened, and she could tell she'd surprised him, by the slow, annoying smile that curled his upper lip. "Don't you think I'm starving, too? It's almost 10:00 p.m.! I haven't eaten since noon." Eyes burning angrily, she took a step toward him.

"Why not?"

"Because I was waiting for you, you big jerk! I've been waiting for you for an entire week now, though heaven only knows why. I'd have walked off this stupid job the first day if it wasn't for my...my..." Much to her mortification, she could feel tears beginning to prick the backs of her eyes. "Never mind." She couldn't let him know how much she needed this job. Somebody born with a silver spoon in his mouth could never really understand the value of a precious, hard-earned dollar. Her chin trembled. *Relax. Regroup. Relax,* she commanded herself and took a cleansing breath.

Out with the unproductive anger.

In with the productive calm.

"I don't recall asking you to starve yourself on my account."

Okay, out with the productive calm. "I was hired to do a *job!* I'm just trying…*to…do my job!*" she shouted, then promptly—and most unprofessionally—burst into tears. Horror-stricken at her undignified behavior, she buried her face behind a stack of handouts.

"Awww, sheez…"

Boots clomping noisily, Bru closed the space between them, and gently grasped her wrist. She could feel him trying to pry her handouts away from her face. Resisting him, she turned away. Mascara was no doubt raining down her cheeks by now, she thought in humiliation as she swiped at the waterworks with the ends of her ever-present bow tie.

"Hey," he whispered, still touching her elbow. "Awww, honey, don't cry." There was something in his voice, something she hadn't heard before. A note of compassion. Understanding. Sympathy. He sounded almost human.

Well, she didn't want his blasted pity, she thought churlishly. She wanted his respect. And she certainly wouldn't get it by standing here blubbering like a baby. She avoided making eye contact with him, knowing that if she did, she might end up throwing herself against his chest and crying her pent-up frustration all over his shirt. No doubt she looked awful. Her nose always turned bright red when she cried. It was a Wainright tradition.

Reaching into his hip pocket, Bru fished out a clean, monogrammed handkerchief and passed it to her. Gratefully she accepted, dabbing and mopping and blowing until she began to feel almost presentable again. The handkerchief was soft against her heated skin and smelled of leather and denim and something spicy and exciting and wonderful, just like him. As she tried to pull herself together, she felt his hands slide from her elbows to her shoulders, and he began to knead the muscles at the nape of her neck, gently easing the tension away. Much to her annoyance, it felt heavenly, and she found herself relaxing against his soothing hands.

"How about if I make it up to you by taking you out to dinner?" he asked. His deep, velvety voice, edged with a slight drawl, was soft in her ear. She could feel him peering over her shoulder at her face. "My treat. You can go over these lessons of yours," he added cajolingly, nodding at the handouts and lesson plans she cradled in her arms.

Fingers probing most deliciously, he continued to dissolve the anxiety that had taken up residence at the base of her neck. *Ummm.* Luckily, she caught herself before she allowed her head to loll back and a moan of rapture to escape her lips.

"I've...l—l—" she lifted her hand and sniffed into his handkerchief "—lost...my appetite," she declared, knowing she sounded every bit as petulant as she felt. As if on cue, her stomach rumbled most embarrassingly, and she winced. Would this humiliating torture never end? What had happened to the cool, sophisticated woman who arrived on Monday morning?

"Yeah. Sure. You've lost your appetite." Gripping her shoulders, Penelope suddenly felt herself being propelled down the stairs and toward his truck. "Come on," he urged, hustling her across the lawn, his arm now firmly locked around her waist.

"Wh-where are we going?"

"Out to dinner."

"But why?" she asked, her eyes, watery pools of blue, blinking up at him.

Heck if he knew. Something about Miss Penelope Wainright had him abandoning his resolve to steer clear of her left and right. Criminy. Only this morning, he'd vowed to stay in town till after midnight, just to avoid her, and yet here he was, forcing her to have a meal with him. Something was definitely wrong with him lately.

"Wouldn't it be quicker and easier to grab something from the kitchen?" she babbled, gesturing blindly toward the house.

Yes. Quicker and easier and a whole lot safer. But Bru didn't like things easy and safe. Opening the passenger door for her, he grasped her slender waist, lifted her onto the running board and nudged her inside. "You sure ask a lot of questions," he grumbled and, before she could retort, slammed the door.

If Bru thought that taking Penelope Wainright to The Rib-O-Rama down at the truck stop just outside a small town in Texas would loosen her up, he'd been wrong. Though she sported a dash of rib sauce on her cheek and her normally tight little bun was beginning to slip, she continued to wield her stiff-necked professionalism like a club. That, and the knife she brandished every time she drove home a point about the importance of image.

Did she ever simply relax? he wondered, watching with great curiosity as she carefully carved the barbecued meat away from the bone and then, cutting it into tiny pieces, proceeded to eat it with a fork. It was an amazing, time-consuming process. And that didn't even take into consideration all the time she spent chewing and dabbing daintily at her lips.

He, on the other hand, used both hands to tackle his pile of ribs, occasionally wiping his fingers—and his face—on the paper bib the waitress had fastened around his neck. No doubt his current table manners were not meeting up with her rigid social expectations, but that was her problem. Licking his fingers, he grinned, remembering the look on her face when the waitress had approached her and unfurled the colorful bib with a showy snap. Yep. Old Penelope had been decidedly uncomfortable with the idea of wearing a bib. Probably, Bru figured in amusement, because she couldn't tie it into one of those infernal bows.

No, indeedy. Bru wasn't exactly sure why he'd brought her to this noisy, smoke-filled greasy spoon perched at the edge of a roaring freeway, other than to further his mission to get Penelope to admit he was a lost cause.

Although, persistent as she was, that might be easier said than done. Well, she may be tough, but he was tougher. She'd have to throw in the towel on him sooner or later. This time, *he* would emerge victorious in this father-son battle of wills. And if Wainright Image Consulting got in the way, well, that was the breaks.

On the other hand, he didn't really want to hurt this driven, controlled woman, with her undying sense of responsibility toward her job and family. Man, he thought, beginning to feel like a real louse. She *would* have to be supporting an ailing mother and a kid brother. Made it kind of hard to do what he had to do.

Not to mention completely and totally exasperating.

"Why don't you just pick it up?" he asked on a beleaguered note, referring to the rib she was chasing around her plate with her fork.

Pausing, she looked up at him and blushed. "Oh, no, thank you," she said, primly declining his advice.

"Why not?"

"Well, uh..." Lifting her shoulders, she studied her plate, her manicure, and her bib as it lay tidily in her lap. "I don't know. I've never tried, I guess."

"Why not?"

"I guess because when I go out to dinner, I'm always with a client,"

"Don't you ever just go out for fun?"

"No."

"Oh, come on." Giving his head an incredulous shake, he allowed his eyes to stray to the gentle curve of her lips. "You never go out to dinner unless you're toting a client? That's unreal."

Her eyes sparked defensively. "Not really. In my situation, it's simpler and less expensive to just...stay in." Blushing, she suddenly looked fascinated by her untouched pile of curly fries.

Somehow, he'd managed to hit a sore spot with her, and instead of feeling triumphant over his complete lack of tact and sensitivity, he felt bad. Shoot. He didn't want to hurt her feelings. He just wanted her to quit. The sooner the better, he thought, as he fought the urge to wipe away the streak of sauce that graced her soft porcelain cheek with his napkin. Somehow, she'd managed to find the chink in his armor. Wouldn't his father jump for joy if he knew how this woman affected him?

He admired her. He didn't want to admire her.

"You gonna eat these?" he asked, snagging several of the untouched curly fries from her plate and stuffing them into his mouth. He hoped he was grossing her out.

"No." She sighed and slid her plate across the table so that he could reach it. "I'm finished. It was delicious," she said, raising her lashes in that slow, mind-numbing way she had of pinning him to the back of his chair with her translucent blue eyes.

Man, he thought, unable to tear his eyes from their mesmerizing grip as he slowly dealt with his mouthful of fries. Never in all his wild days had he encountered eyes like those. When they tangled with his that way, it left him winded. And not much left him winded anymore. No, Bru was the typical guy who had everything. It took something pretty doggone exciting to steal his breath.

Not some stuffy little image consultant like Penelope. No way. Exciting? Nah. He must be hallucinating.

Somewhere in the background, a country-and-western band struck up a rousing ditty that Bru barely noticed.

"Would you care to dance?"

Tearing his gaze from Penelope's, Bru darted a look at the lonely trucker hovering at her elbow and looking hopefully down at her. Bru swallowed and frowned. For Pete's sake, what was he? Invisible? Must be losing his touch, if some yahoo felt comfortable asking his dinner date to dance.

"No," Bru said, sending this social clod a warning look.

"Wasn't askin' you, boy," the potbellied trucker responded, with a brief, irritated glance in Bru's direction, before training his soulful gaze on Penelope. "I was askin' the little lady." He inclined his head respectfully.

Suddenly, a fierce, uncontrollable wave of possessiveness swept over Bru, catching him off guard. No way could he allow someone as delicate and refined as Penelope Wainright to dance with this stranger. Miss Clarise would have his head. Besides, she was his. Maybe not his woman, exactly, but she was with him tonight, nonetheless, and it was his duty to protect her.

"The little lady is with me. If she decides to dance tonight, it will be with me." His voice deadly, Bru pushed back his chair and stood. Lean and lanky, he towered over the burly intruder.

"Why don't you let the little gal speak for herself?" the trucker asked, seeming equally eager to rumble. He took a menacing step toward Bru and hiked his pants back up around his waist.

The tension was suddenly so thick, Bru could have cut it with a rib. He didn't want to have to punch this guy out, but he would if he had to.

"Thank you very much," Penelope interjected, ever winning friends and influencing people. Even idiots like this dolt, Bru thought with disgust. "But," she said kindly, "I'm not much of a dancer. I'm flattered that you asked, though." Her smile warm, she nodded and extended her hand.

Bru thought he would loose his rib dinner—curly fries and all—as the trucker gallantly grasped her fingers and smeared his greasy lips across the back of her hand.

"Walll, now," the trucker drawled, mollified by her personable demeanor, "maybe another time." With a scowl at Bru, he shuffled off into the crowd in search of more available prey.

"I should have decked him," Bru muttered, sinking back into his chair.

"Why?"

"For being an idiot."

"What good would that have done?" Penelope stared at him, clearly stymied by his rather physical approach to influencing people.

"It would have taught him a lesson."

"What lesson?" Penelope's brows knotted in confusion. "Don't you know that you can catch far more flies with honey than with vinegar?"

Bru snorted in the direction the trucker had retreated. "Who wants to catch him?"

Her brow knit in consternation. "You just don't get it, do you?"

Aww, geez. Rearing back in his seat, he dragged his hands across his face and groaned. She was off on one of her blasted image jags again. He was getting pretty tired of her holier-than-thou attitude when it came to business. For crying out loud, he'd single-handedly—the times Big Daddy would butt out—run one of the world's biggest corporations, and here she was, some know-it-all consultant, telling him what to do. It blew his mind.

"Listen, Penelope, as much as it may surprise you, I have been around the professional-glad-handing-nicey-nice block a time or two. You don't have the corner on professional style, you know. I may be a little rough around the edges after spending so much time out on the range with the dunderheads who work for me, but down at the corporate offices, I know my way around the boardroom. I could step back into my position without missing a beat."

Her skeptical expression irritated him beyond belief.

Leaning forward, he pushed his plate out of the way and tapped the tabletop with his forefinger. "You seem to think I ran Brubaker International from the back of my horse.

Well, let me tell you, technology may have come a long way, but they still haven't figured out how to get a saddle horn to double as a fax machine. Yes, once in a while I had to step into the office to cut a deal. And you know what? I did just fine.'' As he slapped the table to emphasize his point, he had to wonder why he was going out of his way to convince her. He had to wonder why he was acting so defensive.

Taking a deep breath of the smoky Rib-O-Rama air, he exhaled heavily, disgusted with himself. Nobody loved Big Daddy more than Bru did, but at times like this he had to wonder why—if his father drove him so crazy—he was bound and determined to act just like him. They were cut from the same cloth, he and Big Daddy. And there was a competitive spirit between father and eldest son that neither of them seemed able to control.

Eyes lowered, Penelope began to unbutton her cuffs and roll up her sleeves. ''Mind if I ask you a personal question?'' she asked. Thoughtfully she raised her gaze to his face.

''You and your questions.'' He sighed and shrugged. What was one more question he couldn't answer? ''Shoot.''

''If everything was so fine, why did you walk off the job?''

He'd been wondering when she'd finally get around to asking. Cupping his cheek in the palm of his hand, Bru angled his head and studied her through eyes that looked back across his career. ''Because my father wasn't ready to retire. To turn the business over to me. And I was tired of fighting him.''

Folding her arms, she rested them lightly on the tabletop. ''Don't you think you might be able to benefit from your father's experience?''

''I learned everything I know about business from watching my father at work. He's brilliant. That's not the point.''

"Okay, if he's so brilliant, what difference does it make if he sticks his nose in the business every once in a while?"

"If it was only every once in a while, that would be one thing. Every five minutes…well, I have to wonder what he needs me for."

"Maybe at this stage of the game, your needs aren't important. Perhaps it's your father who simply needs to feel needed."

Bru snorted. Now she was psychoanalyzing him and his father. "We've *all* figured that out."

"Then I guess I don't understand why you fight him this way. Wouldn't it be easier to simply do as he asks? To work on your image and eventually step back into your place at Brubaker International?"

It was clear she didn't understand. Not having grown up a Brubaker, she probably never would. Explaining their family dynamic to her could take all night. And if he was going to spend the night talking to Penelope, it sure as heck wasn't going to be about his wacky relationship with Big Daddy. He wished she'd just give up and quit trying to change him. He wished she'd just quit. Period.

"I like working the ranch. I like the horses, the cattle, the land. I like everything just fine the way it is."

"Are you sure you don't like working the ranch so much because it irritates your father?" She reached out and, seemingly unconsciously, grasped his hand. "Oh, Bru, you're far too young to be so obstinate when it comes to working with Big Daddy. Just because you successfully ran Brubaker International for two years doesn't mean you can't learn anything from your father anymore."

He studied her slender hand as it lay twined in his larger, rougher one. Did she have any idea what she was doing to his blood pressure? "Penelope, I know you mean well, but you just don't understand what it's like to work for my father. It's frustrating as hell."

A brilliant smile lit her face, transforming her from high-powered business woman to...woman. "Hey. I've been working for him for a week now. No offense, but this is the most frustrating job I've ever taken."

He grinned in spite of himself. Lordy, she had beautiful eyes. So blue, if he had wings, he could have flown in them. "Touché," he murmured, grateful for the break in this tense conversation. He hated analyzing his relationship with his father. Made him feel nuttier than a squirrel at harvesttime.

Seeming to realize this, Penelope changed the subject. "So. Are you going to stand me up Saturday night?" she asked, darting him a look that was surprisingly impish, for someone so bent on behaving like a robot.

"What's happening Saturday night?"

She groaned. "You've forgotten already?"

No. He hadn't. In fact, he'd done nothing that entire afternoon but think about taking her out Saturday night. He was looking forward to taking her out. And for that very reason he needed to get out of taking her out. "The CIA party?" he asked, stalling.

"Close enough. Are you going or not?"

Something akin to a vise clamped down on his guts, deep in his belly, as he watched the way she nervously chewed on her lower lip. What was it about her that had him acting like a hormone-driven teenager? His feelings toward her had run the gamut from dislike to admiration, and he'd only known her a week. He had to get control of these wayward emotions. He had to stop spending time with her. He had to stop noticing the way she filled out that frumpy little swimsuit of hers. Barely conscious that his lips were moving, he suddenly heard himself respond.

"Yes."

"Really?" She fairly beamed with delight.

"Really." What an idiot. Well, he'd repent at leisure over this decision. In the meantime, maybe he could figure out a way to turn this CIA ordeal in his favor. Maybe, just maybe, this party would be the ticket to getting rid of Penelope.

And getting Big Daddy off his back.

Later that evening, back at the house, Bru walked Penelope down the wide upstairs corridor that led to their suites. It was late, and he figured everyone must have turned in for the night. It seemed strange, walking his date to her door at the end of the evening, and having that door be just down the hall from his own. Strange, he mused, but convenient. Besides, this wasn't a date. He had to get that through his head. Penelope was the enemy.

Why hadn't he realized that the enemy could be so compelling? Suddenly uneasy in his own skin, Bru wrestled with this dilemma, his eyes straying of their own accord to her lovely face as they arrived at the double doors that led to her room.

He slowed, wondering what sort of etiquette she would expect by way of a professional, image-related good-night. Half of him wanted to keep on walking till he reached his door, then disappear inside without so much as a see-ya-later. The other half of him wanted to grab her and finally give in to the tension he'd felt building deep in his belly since the moment he'd first laid eyes on her. He'd come so close to kissing her so many times, he feared he'd lose his mind if he didn't give up and let it happen.

But he couldn't. Kissing the enemy would mean certain victory for his father. Silently he cursed the situation, wishing that she was just another woman in his long list of dance partners down at The Jubilee Truckstop. Then he could kiss her without guilt. The slight dash of rib sauce still adorned her silky cheek. It would be the perfect excuse to touch her. To taste her. The well-rehearsed lines he could use on her flashed through his mind.

But he couldn't.

He shouldn't.

Wouldn't.

Grabbing her elbow, he pulled her up short, before her door. A single step closed the distance between them, and when she lifted her face to his, he thought his knees had turned to water. As his eyes stabbed into hers, his heart roared in his ears and his ragged breath came in short, labored puffs. For an infinitesimal moment, his lips hovered just shy of hers as he struggled against a pull so strong, it threatened to strangle him with its intensity. He was shaking, for the love of Mike. Bru Brubaker never shook.

"Good night," he rasped. Releasing her elbow, he gave her hand a professional pump. Then, before his resolve flagged and he gave in to his baser instincts, Bru strode down the hall to his room, yanked open the door and, with a resounding crash, disappeared for the night.

"Darn." Penelope sighed, lightly running her fingertips across her lower lip. She'd forgotten to tell him he was supposed to bring a date tomorrow night. Her eyes flitted from her door to his.

He would still be awake.

She would just run down there and tell him the part about the date. Of course, the fact that it would give him just one more chance to kiss her good-night never entered her mind.

Chapter Six

Leaning against his bedroom door, Bru closed his eyes tightly and groaned. *That was close.* He waited for his rapid breathing to slow and his blood pressure to fall. Score one for him, he thought with a tired sigh. This private little war he was waging with his father was turning out to be more challenging than he'd ever anticipated. Then again, how could he have known that his father would toss him a Molotov cocktail in the form of one persistent yet professional and perky...Penelope? A slow smile eased the tension at the corners of his mouth. He had to give Big Daddy points for coming up with her.

Exhaling heavily, he opened his eyes and allowed his gaze to travel around his disheveled room, and was suddenly chagrined. He couldn't believe that someone as superorganized and tidy as Penelope had been in here. Bru didn't like anyone to see his room this way. Not even the maids. Yup. It was time to clean up. Either that, or a take a long, very chilly shower. Arching his back, he pushed away from the door and studied the project with a critical eye. Not pretty. But, hell, he'd been angry. Probably a little more angry than he'd been willing to admit over having to relinquish his position down at Brubaker International. His stepping down had been necessary, but that didn't mean it had been easy.

Muscles working in his jaw, he decided that cleaning up might help him begin to put the whole ordeal in the past, where it belonged. Exorcise some of his demons. Get that fresh start Penelope liked to jabber on about. Grabbing an armful of clothes off the floor, he tossed them into a laundry basket and kicked it over to the door. Then, with a savage grunt, he upended his bed and began to root out things from beneath the box spring that he hadn't seen in a month of Sundays.

"Mmm…" he mused as he paused for a moment in the midst his cleaning frenzy, "…so *that's* where those shoes went…." He fired the shiny wing tips over his shoulder and into the closet.

It was a grudge match. Bru against his room. Bru against his father. Bru against the separate worlds of business and ranching. Bru against the lure of a pair of the most hypnotic blue eyes he'd ever seen. Maybe, he thought, huffing and puffing as he moved from the chaos under his bed to open an antique armoire that he hadn't opened in months, just maybe, if he worked hard enough, he could drive those big baby blues out of his mind. Maybe he'd even be able to get a decent night's sleep.

Nah. If he'd had more than five consecutive minutes that entire week when she hadn't taken his thought processes by storm, he'd eat his Stetson. Pausing in his efforts to force open the armoire's jammed door, he frowned. Locked? For a moment, he grappled with the antique key and wondered absently what would happen if he simply took her damnable lessons and got them over with and sent her on her merry way. As much as he was reluctant to admit it, he could probably use a refresher course. Hanging out with Red and Fuzzy and the rest of those ranch hands certainly hadn't done much for his corporate image.

He'd been away from the world of big business for three long years now.

Tired of fighting the blasted door to the armoire, Bru looked around. What had he done with his gun? It was probably under a stack of something or another. On second thought, better not. Miss Clarise would blow a gasket if he shot an antique. Especially inside the house.

Had it really been three years? Already?

Suddenly, Bru felt a restless burning to get back in the business saddle and take charge of the corporation.

With a monumental effort, he squelched it. Why cry over spilt milk?

Ripping his shirt off over his head, Bru mopped his face, then flung it into the laundry basket. After a quick perusal of his nightstand he grabbed a mallard-shaped brass bookend and viciously attacked the knob of the armoire's door with its beak.

No, he thought, grunting as he pecked away with his bookend, as much as he might enjoy the time spent in her company, he couldn't let himself graduate from Penelope's image class. It was a matter of principle. And he also knew that as long as his father was still letting him drive the corporate empire only to grab the wheel back when they came to a curve in the road of business, he couldn't go back to Brubaker International. The constant bickering and fighting had nearly killed his mother. Besides, he thought, as he merely succeeded in bending the brass bird's beak with the stubborn doorknob, going back would send his father the message that he was the kind of man someone could run roughshod over.

And nobody ran roughshod over Bru Brubaker.

Not even a persnickety, workaholic, loyal-to-a-fault, leggy, full-lipped, porcelain-skinned, wavy-haired pain in the neck like Penelope. Growling, he tossed the mallard over his shoulder and kicked at the door.

He should have kissed her when he had the chance. He should have grabbed her right then and there and kissed

NO COST! NO OBLIGATION TO BUY!
NO PURCHASE NECESSARY!

PLAY "LUCKY 7"
AND GET FIVE FREE GIFTS!

HOW TO PLAY:

1. With a coin, carefully scratch off the silver box at the right. Then check the claim chart to see what we have for you—FREE BOOKS and a gift—ALL YOURS! ALL FREE!

2. Send back this card and you'll receive brand-new Silhouette Romance™ novels. These books have a cover price of $3.25 each, but they are yours to keep absolutely free.

3. There's no catch. You're under no obligation to buy anything. We charge nothing—ZERO—for your first shipment. And you don't have to make any minimum number of purchases—not even one!

4. The fact is thousands of readers enjoy receiving books by mail from the Silhouette Reader Service™ months before they're available in stores. They like the convenience of home delivery and they love our discount prices!

5. We hope that after receiving your free books you'll want to remain a subscriber. But the choice is yours—to continue or cancel, anytime at all! So why not take us up on our invitation, with no risk of any kind. You'll be glad you did!

MISS PRIM'S UNTAMABLE COWBOY

as a dangerous look. A look of frustration. Of
...owering her hand from where she'd touched his
swallowed and willed her feet to carry her down
...oward the safe haven of her room. But they were
...nt feet. She blinked, attempting to tear her eyes
...m his bare chest as it rose and fell above his
...ungs.

...s this was not such a good idea, she thought, and
... same time unable to stop herself from wonder-
...it would feel like if he dragged her into his arms
... her senseless. His skin looked so warm. So soft.
...g, in a steely, hard, animal kind of way. Slowly
...ed her eyes to his, and as their eyes collided, the
...hed from her lungs and she stood rooted to her
...ly capable of breathing.

...ional, she told herself and inhaled deeply. *Re-*
...you are a professional.

...ted to tell you... Uh, you need to know that...''
...?''

...tumbled over each other in a heated rush. "You
...sk a date to the party Saturday night.''

...frown marred his brow as he puzzled over the
...f her words. "A date?''

...ared her throat. "Yes.'' It was so awkward,
...here, staring at him, this shirtless demolition
...o seemed—for some inexplicable reason—hell-
...stroying his bedroom. Her eyes strayed over his
...ulder passed the double doors and into his suite.
...just cleaning.''

...She tried to think of something to say. Some-
...sounded casual. Something pertaining to busi-
...his date. But she could think of nothing except
...vished he would sweep her off her feet, carry her
...hallway and into the land of happily-ever-after.
...scible Bru Brubaker was her fairy-tale prince?
...vas really losing it. She was also incredibly, un-
..., tempted by him. Unfortunately, he was off-

her till that streak of barbecue sa
tasty memory. He should have pre
ows of the hallway, pulled off her
up her no-nonsense bun and had h
oxygen. He should have dragged h
arms and plundered her mouth wit
for mercy.

Or begged for more.

Heart pounding, lungs panting, B
knob and braced his foot agains
cherrywood. Twisting for all he w
bulged as he gave the old door a n

The ensuing avalanche had Bru

Whatever had possessed him to
shelf of an antique armoire?

Hearing the crash from beyon
paused just short of knocking. Was
she thought as the pithy expletives
delicate ears, he seemed upset abo
her fingertips against the door, she

Maybe she should just tell him i
he would have time to invite a date
night. True, it was short notice,
Thursday, he had all day tomorrow

Another crash.

Yes. She should leave, she deci
step backward.

Although…he should know that
However…she didn't want to nag
again…Big Daddy was paying he
classes, and part of the class was th
other hand…Bru didn't want to tak

Although…he did need the exper
She knocked. A light rap. Barely
Expression wild, Bru threw open
The look in his eyes had her hear

ribs. It
passion.
door, sh
the hall
disobed
away fr
heaving

Perha
was at t
ing wha
and kiss
So invi
she dra
air who
spot, ba

Profe
member

"I w

"Wh
Word
need to

A tir
meanin

She
standin
derby
bent or
broad s

"I w

"Oh
thing t
ness. T
how sh
down

The
Ha! Sh
mercif

limits for so many reasons. She was working for Mr. Brubaker, and she needed to remember that. With a single
word, Big Daddy Brubaker could make or break her career.
Besides, she knew deep in her soul, that she was not Bru's
type. He liked his women experienced. Worldly. Fast and
wild. The same way he liked to drive.

The wildest thing Penelope had ever done was wait till
just before midnight on April 15 to mail her income tax
returns. That would probably not tempt a virile specimen
like Bru to take her in his arms and give her the kiss she
was dying for.

An endless number of ticks tocked on the stately grand-
father clock that was situated at the end of the hall near
the back stairs. They stood there for what seemed to both
of them like an eon, not speaking, staring at each other,
fighting urges, battling frustration and warring with this
primal tension that neither could admit to the other.

"You want me to ask a date."

"To the ICAA party Saturday night. Yes."

He didn't blink. "No problem."

Penelope was devastated. She hated the idea of spending
the evening with him and another woman. "Good." A
little sigh escaped her lips. "Well, I should probably be
going."

"Probably," he said. He sounded strained.

"I'll see you tomorrow night, for the lesson. I'll wait
for you in the gazebo. Eight o'clock okay?"

Bru continued to probe her with his brooding stare for
so long, she began to fear something was the matter with
him. His fists opened and closed at his sides, his pupils
were dilated, his breathing erratic.

"Penelope?" He ground out her name through his
tightly clenched jaw.

"Yes," she breathed, feeling faint as he reached for her.

"You have rib sauce on your cheek."

"How's it goin'?"

Penelope looked up from her course materials and

smiled at Big Daddy's cheerful face. Climbing up into the gazebo where she was sitting, the diminutive man settled himself in the swing opposite her and pinned her with his crinkly, raisinlike gaze.

With a covert glance at her watch, she debated whether or not to admit she'd been planning his eldest son's homicide. No. Bru was late for his eight-o'clock session, but he wasn't that late. Yet.

"Fine," she lied. Goodness. She was becoming so adept at avoiding the truth. Just that morning, she'd given her mother the same song and dance about how ducky her project was going out here at the Circle B.O. But she'd fibbed for her mother's sake. Her mother had enough on her plate without worrying about her daughter's crumbling career. Suddenly—as she returned Big Daddy's smile— she missed her own family.

It hadn't even been quite a week yet that she'd been gone, but it seemed like a lifetime. Randy had been going off to baseball practice every afternoon, and was becoming one of the team's best pitchers. Aunt Geraldine was enjoying her stay, and the two sisters had been giggling and gossiping the days away.

Why, they barely even knew she was gone, her mother had assured her. Penelope was certain her mother had only been trying to ease her mind, but nevertheless, it made her feel dispensable. And lately, that was how she felt all the time. Completely and utterly dispensable.

It seemed the doctor had finally scheduled her mother's hip-replacement surgery. "Isn't that wonderful?" her mother had enthused across the lines. "I'll be up and around in no time."

No time. The words echoed dismally in Penelope's head. The time just kept tick-tick-ticking away, and still she was no closer than the day she'd arrived to polishing Bru's deplorable image. How would she pay the mounting bills? Gripping the arm of her swing, Penelope ground her teeth in determination. She had to succeed in this project of Big Daddy's. Somehow, she had to come up with a way to outsmart Bru, she decided as she watched Big Daddy slam his back against the giant swing, gleefully setting it in motion. She had to think of a way to beat Bru at his own game. In ways she didn't fully understand, Penelope almost relished the challenge. Competitive spirit was no stranger to the Wainrights. Although this was one of the most maddening games she'd ever played.

And, at the same time, one of the most exhilarating. Yes, she thought as a sense of purpose surged through her veins, somehow she would figure out a way to tame the beast and at the same time earn her much-needed bonus. The national anthem swelled in her head as she took her gold-medal bows in her mind's eye.

"Yes, sir," she said with a triumphant smile, "everything is going just fine."

"Well, now, *good!* That's the spirit," Big Daddy crowed, beaming. Dragging his tiny boots on the wooden floor of the gazebo, Big Daddy stopped the swaying motion of his swing and leaned forward conspiratorially. "In that case, I want Bru to take over his old job down at Brubaker International headquarters sooner than we'd planned."

"Oh?" Penelope nodded serenely, hoping to belie that sudden drumroll of her heart. Sooner than we'd planned? Her buoyant mood began to sink.

"Here's the deal," Big Daddy continued, heaping coals onto the smoldering embers of her anxiety. "With you being so confident and all about being able to whip that boy of mine into shape, I'm going ahead with my plans to take the little missus on a round-the-world thirty-second anniversary honeymoon trip. Shh." Pressing his finger to his wide grin, he winked at her. "It's a secret, so don't breathe a word."

"Uh...okay."

"Anywho, I need Bru at the helm before the end of the

summer. We will be gone for several months. Then, when we get back, I have some other—'' he paused and squinted at her ''—very important 'projects' to pursue that have nothin' to do with business. Family stuff. That bein' the case, I can't be bothered with runnin' Brubaker International anymore. I want out. For good. The end. Kaput.'' He grinned. ''You get the idea.''

''Yes.'' Penelope smiled weakly as the import of his words came crashing down around her. If Bru wasn't ready for work before the end of the summer, this darling little man couldn't take his anniversary trip with Miss Clarise. Her stomach began to churn. She needed time to digest this latest news, in order to take it in her professional stride. Taking a deep breath, she blinked away the pinpoints of light that danced before her eyes. She would be fine in a moment. Hopefully.

Smiling, Penelope attempted to shake off her fears. She was up to the task. She was a Wainright, after all. Big Daddy was such a sweetie, if she could, she would give him the moon. Why, she wondered sadly, wasn't Bru able to see what a wonderful father he had?

''I need you to concentrate on Bru till he shines like a new copper penny.''

''Okay…'' Before it had even begun, her career was going up in smoke. She sighed.

''Because before you can say 'head honcho,' he'll be filling my shoes.'' Big Daddy held up his minuscule boot and laughed. ''Ya know, I don't know how I evah ended up with such huge kids. Must be the fresh ranch air, or maybe the truckloads of food I feed 'em…''

As quickly as it had come over her, Penelope's brief fit of melancholy began to dissipate at Big Daddy's silly antics. Something about his total confidence in her abilities relaxed her. Gave her hope. Laughter swept them both away, and together they enjoyed a moment of easy camaraderie.

* * *

Bru paused in the shadows of several old live oak trees, and observed his father and Penelope indulging in some lighthearted teasing. A pang of unexpected jealousy zinged through his gut. He wished he could simply spend a few carefree moments in her company, no matter how counterproductive that would be to his goal.

Big Daddy really seemed to like her. The gentle peck his father planted on her forehead as he bid her good-night did not go unnoticed by Bru. Dagnabbit anyway, he thought disgruntledly, why should the old man get to kiss her, and not him? Then again, kissing the enemy was never a good tactical maneuver.

"'Night, now, sugar doll," Big Daddy called jauntily over his shoulder as he exited the gazebo and strolled toward the house.

"'Night, Big Daddy," she returned.

Emerging from the thick foliage of the live oaks, Bru glanced at his watch and headed across the lawn toward Penelope. He figured he might as well take his lumps and get it over with. After all, he had promised to attend her party tomorrow night, and this evening had been their last chance to go over some of the course material that she claimed would get a cowpoke like him over this particular hurdle in the course. He snorted. Just wait till she got a load of his contingency plan.

"You're two hours late." Penelope sighed, not bothering to look up from the impressive stack of course materials she had cradled in her arms.

How had she known he was there? His eyes widened. She was good. Formidable. An appreciative grin tugged his mouth. He liked that in an opponent. Bounding up to the gazebo, he took the steps two at a time and threw himself into the swing she occupied. Suddenly he was in a buoyant mood. Which was odd, considering that his day had been the pits.

"Don't be mad," he implored her, pulling out his standard brand of boyish vulnerability, coupled with the little

Elvis-type curl of his upper lip that was meant to lull her into a false sense of security. It never failed to charm the socks off the women in his life. "And stop worrying about the party. I'll wing it. I have some experience at conducting myself in public, you know," he assured her. He'd worry about his public-conduct game plan tomorrow. Right now, he just wanted to sit next to her and enjoy the moonlight.

Penelope harrumphed grumpily, seemingly impervious to his charm. "At least do me the favor of going over your notes." She lobbed the ream of paper—which had to weigh a good five pounds—into his lap.

"Okay." He shrugged. Why not? With her sleeping in a bed just a door or two down the hall, he wouldn't be getting much shut-eye, anyway.

"Did you remember to ask a date?"

He hung his head and hoped he looked dejected. "Yes." Which was true enough. He had remembered. He simply hadn't bothered. "But, unfortunately, they all had other plans." Also true. Every eligible woman he knew would be dancing Saturday night away down at The Jubilee Truckstop. Bru darted a soulful glance in her direction.

Penelope paused and swallowed, then took a deep breath. "Fine," she retorted, jiggling the swing dramatically as she stood and strode across the gazebo. Turning, she faced him for a moment. "In that case, you are just going to have to attend the party with me as your date."

"Whatever you say, teach," he deadpanned, attempting to stifle the giddy, kidlike feeling that welled into his throat at the prospect of an evening alone with her. "Hey, where are you going?" He sat up, suddenly realizing she was leaving. "I thought we had a class tonight," he called after her as she descended the gazebo's steps.

"Class is dismissed, Mr. Brubaker. You're on your own." With a toss of her head, she spun on her heel and was gone.

Bru looked at the course materials in his lap. "Better

get to work,'' he muttered. He needed to arm himself if he was going to win the war.

Bru felt his mouth go dry as he helped Penelope—one long, shapely leg at a time—gracefully exit the limo Big Daddy had loaned them for the occasion. Even in her sedate, plain black evening dress, she was a knockout. It was amazing how, with a such modest neckline, a simple strand of pearls and a hemline that wafted enticingly down around her calves, she could look so completely fetching.

This evening, she wore her hair piled loosely at her crown, in a less severe version of her daily bun. And, he suddenly realized, grinning at the irony, it was the first time he ever seen her without one of her infernal bows knotted at her throat. Tonight, it would seem, *he* was the one doomed to wear the bow tie. Adjusting the uncomfortable knot, he followed Penelope through the double doors and across the foyer of the elegant old St. Marquis Hotel in downtown Dallas.

Apparently Penelope had been to the old hotel's Grand Ballroom on several occasions, because she seemed to know her way around this building as she led him to the tastefully decorated area where her colleagues were beginning to gather. With a cheerful wave at several people she knew, she slipped her hand into the crook of Bru's elbow and drew him aside.

"Before we get started, I want to take a second and run to the powder room to check my makeup," she whispered.

Tipping her chin up with his forefinger, Bru allowed his gaze to wander slowly over her face. "Why? I think you look fine."

"This coming from a man who let me spend an entire evening with a blob of barbecue sauce on my cheek." Brows high, she narrowed her gaze at him.

"On you, it looked good." He meant it.

She rolled her eyes. "I'll be back in a minute."

"I'll be here." He waved her on.

Sighing, she breathed, "I hope so."

Yes, well, she might change her mind before the evening was over, he thought ruefully. He had a mission to accomplish this evening, and he wasn't planning on taking any prisoners. By the end of the night, if he played his cards right, Penelope would be begging his father to take her resignation. The idea gave his conscience a bit of a pang. Resolutely he brushed it away.

Taking up his post just outside the Grand Ballroom, he leaned casually against the wall, giving himself a chance to familiarize himself with the surroundings. To get the lay of the land so to speak.

Let's see... Last night he'd burned the midnight oil reviewing Penelope's course materials and filing some of the more pertinent image information in the back of his mind. He would try to hit all the highlights tonight, he thought smugly as he allowed his memory to visualize and scan the course materials in his mind's eye.

Hmmm... Techniques for a successful social situation included proper attire...eye contact... Listen attentively... Make people feel important... Appreciate accomplishments... Avoid loud and vexing behavior... Avoid arguments... Admit you're wrong... Exude friendship... Sympathize... Respect others' opinions... Praise... Taking command with leading questions... Telephone technique...? No, not pertinent...

As Bru mentally reviewed the course material, his eyes wandered around the Grand Ballroom. There were more people here than he'd originally anticipated. Already at least fifty people were wandering around the room, putting their newfound behavioral patterns into practice. Never had he seen so much handshaking, proper introduction procedure, smiling and animated chitchat designed to draw one another out. Though he knew it was part of business, just watching these social gyrations made Bru long for his horse.

His eyes swung to the band as it warmed up and began

get to work," he muttered. He needed to arm himself if he was going to win the war.

Bru felt his mouth go dry as he helped Penelope—one long, shapely leg at a time—gracefully exit the limo Big Daddy had loaned them for the occasion. Even in her sedate, plain black evening dress, she was a knockout. It was amazing how, with a such modest neckline, a simple strand of pearls and a hemline that wafted enticingly down around her calves, she could look so completely fetching.

This evening, she wore her hair piled loosely at her crown, in a less severe version of her daily bun. And, he suddenly realized, grinning at the irony, it was the first time he ever seen her without one of her infernal bows knotted at her throat. Tonight, it would seem, *he* was the one doomed to wear the bow tie. Adjusting the uncomfortable knot, he followed Penelope through the double doors and across the foyer of the elegant old St. Marquis Hotel in downtown Dallas.

Apparently Penelope had been to the old hotel's Grand Ballroom on several occasions, because she seemed to know her way around this building as she led him to the tastefully decorated area where her colleagues were beginning to gather. With a cheerful wave at several people she knew, she slipped her hand into the crook of Bru's elbow and drew him aside.

"Before we get started, I want to take a second and run to the powder room to check my makeup," she whispered.

Tipping her chin up with his forefinger, Bru allowed his gaze to wander slowly over her face. "Why? I think you look fine."

"This coming from a man who let me spend an entire evening with a blob of barbecue sauce on my cheek." Brows high, she narrowed her gaze at him.

"On you, it looked good." He meant it.

She rolled her eyes. "I'll be back in a minute."

"I'll be here." He waved her on.

to play some snatches of lively dance-type tunes. Live music and a dance floor. Good. From the band, his gaze swung to the buffet table. Hors d'oeuvres. Perfect.

Tugging at his infernal bow tie, Bru took a deep breath. He guessed he was as ready as he'd ever be. Part of him was exhilarated by the challenge of executing his plan. Part of him was sorry that it had to end this way with the remarkable Penelope. Under different circumstances... Well, he couldn't allow himself to think about that. He was at war with his father. No matter how attracted he might be to Penelope, no matter how much he might like her or respect what she was doing with her life, he couldn't let that interfere with his mission. He had to stay the course.

"All set." Penelope's voice was sweet and low at his shoulder. "Shall we mingle?" She slipped her delicate hand into the crook of his arm.

For a brief moment, he had second thoughts. In the past, it had always made sense to fight fire with fire. When it came to Big Daddy, anyway. But now... He swallowed, his Adam's apple straining against his tie.

"Stay the course," he muttered under his breath. Deciding that there was no time like the present to activate his plan, he stripped the suffocating tie from around his neck and stuffed it into the breast pocket of his tux jacket.

A puzzled frown marred Penelope's brow but, much to her credit, she swallowed her concerns.

"Let's go," he said, his grin engaging. With one hand, he began to unbutton his collar studs, and with the other he pulled her rapidly across the Grand Ballroom floor and passed several people who were obviously testing their newfound skills and trying to make their acquaintance.

"Bru, slow down, I'd like to introduce you to..." Penelope's voice bounced from over his shoulder as she skipped after him and gestured toward the group of eager minglers.

"Hang on, just a sec," Bru called, nodding at his fellow

image students with a jaunty salute. "Hi there. Be right with you."

"Bru, these people want to meet—"

"Yeah, okay, sure. No problem. Give me a second here," he instructed as he tugged a flustered Penelope over to the buffet table, which was loaded with party appetizers. Donning an apologetic expression, he said to her, "I'm sorry, but I didn't get a chance to eat dinner tonight, and my blood sugar is crashing." He hoped his smile was charming. Irresistible. "You don't mind?"

Penelope looked around, obviously aware that her student was the first to tie on the feed bag and feeling awkward about it. "No...I, um, go right ahead." She smiled brightly. "We can't have you fainting from hunger, now, can we?"

Bru arched a contemplative brow. Say, now—he hadn't thought of that. Maybe later. Grabbing a plate, he ambled down the table and loaded it with a handful of everything. "Okay. I'm ready," he said lazily, juggling his overloaded plate, napkins, silverware and punch cup in his hands. "Let's mingle."

Following Penelope toward a pair who beckoned from the corner, he couldn't help but notice that she was easily the most attractive woman in the room. She had the kind of class that everyone else here tonight was paying top dollar for. And to her it came naturally. Admiration swelled in his chest, taking on a life of its own. He hated himself for the fits he'd given her since they met. For the fits he was planning to give her. She didn't deserve this.

Don't go all soft now, old boy, he chided himself. The fact that she had successfully wormed her way into the mushy spot in his heart was just more of Big Daddy's strategy. Bru knew how his father's devious mind worked. Well, he could outdevious his old man any day of the week, he thought determinedly as he leaned over his plate and snagged a crab puff between his teeth.

Mentally he counted on his fingers. So far, he'd flunked

proper appearance and making people feel important. Good. Now he had to stumble over the table-etiquette and introduction hurdles. Before the evening was over, he planned to turn political incorrectness into a high art form.

"Hello, Sue, hello, William," Penelope sang as she made her way toward a rigid pair who stood in the corner like royalty holding court. "I'd like you both to meet my only student this semester." She gestured behind her, toward Bru, and smiled at Sue and William.

In an effort to avoid as much eye contact as possible, Bru ducked his head over his plate, randomly grazing at its contents. Covertly he darted a quick peek at William. Stuffed shirt. His eyes shifted to Sue. Stuffed dress.

"I'm giving a series of private lessons over the summer," Penelope said by way of explanation of the fact that she wasn't in the company of her usual half-dozen students and their dates.

"I see," Sue murmured, her piercing, beady eyes darting an imperious look at the steadily snacking Bru.

"Sue Xena, William Larson, this is…Conway Brubaker." Penelope said pleasantly after shaking their hands.

"Nobody calls me Conway," he growled around his third crab puff.

Cheeks pink, Penelope frowned at him and forged ahead. "Bru is a cattle rancher."

"Oh," Sue said, looking down her pointed nose, a note of disdain creeping into her voice, as she watched him stuff his face.

Penelope stared at him. "Uh, yes," she said when she could finally speak, "Apparently, uh, Bru here suffers from low blood sugar."

"Ah." Noses wrinkled, Sue and William slowly nodded.

"Sue and William are image consultants and co-owners of X-L Image," Penelope explained for Bru's benefit.

Bru choked. Lurch and Morticia were *image* consultants? *They* owned X-L Image?

"Yes indeed." Sue nodded, her gaunt cheeks becoming hollow as she pursed her thin lips. "Ah, and here come some of our students now." She gestured to a group of minglers that were making their way over to them. One at a time she introduced Helen, James, Roy, Edna, and Mary Patricia and their dates in the complex yet proper order of their age, social status and business position.

"Mmmphff," Bru grunted and, leaning forward, snagged a chicken strip with his teeth and slowly lipped it into his mouth. "Mff...good," he mumbled, leaning chummily against the ghoulish Sue. "Mmmm.... You thould try thith little thingamajigth," he said encouragingly, holding his plate out to her. "They're thpicy, though, tho hold on to your hat."

"No, thank you." Sue declined haughtily. "I am a vegetarian."

"No prob. You can have the rest of my celery."

Penelope elbowed him painfully in the ribs. *"Stop it,"* she hissed up at him, all the while smiling at Sue through her clenched jaw.

"What?" Bru arched an innocent brow.

Turning her back on Sue, she clutched his lapel and tugged his ear to her mouth. *"You're embarrassing me."*

Looking down into her mortified eyes, Bru felt gigantic stabs of conscience. How was he going to flawlessly execute his counterattack in this war with his father, with her looking up at him that way? He knew he was being a first-class jerk, but that was the whole idea. All was fair in love and war, wasn't it? As he scanned the worry etched between her brow, he wasn't so sure anymore. He had to get away from those liquid blue pools that looked so imploringly up at him. They were pulling him under. Drowning him in a sea of guilt. *Stay the course,* he cautioned himself. *Execute the plan.* Despite the casualties, he had to win the war.

"I'm sorry," he said, ducking his head contritely.

"Where are my manners?" He held out his plate to her. "Crab puff?"

Mortified, Penelope whirled around, turning her back on Bru, and, with an obviously monumental effort, smiled at Edna and asked her what she did for a living.

She was the consummate professional, Bru thought, admiration for this woman swelling in his chest, becoming just another faction in the internal battle he was waging with himself. Bru had to give her credit. Even in the most dire circumstances, the image she projected was always above reproach.

Unlike himself.

However, Bru thought rebelliously, before he turned into the obedient lapdog that Big Daddy was no doubt paying through the nose for, he had to stem the flow of his bleeding heart. He needed to get away from the well-intentioned Penelope and her hypnotic blue eyes.

Thankfully, the band finished tuning their instruments and launched into a rousing forties-style big-band number. The fact that it was far too early in the party to begin dancing made this his perfect escape route.

"Ah, man, this is my favorite," Bru announced to no one in particular. "Say, Trish—" he sent a beseeching look in the staid Mary Patricia's direction "—would you care to dance?"

Mary Patricia gave her head a tiny shake and took a careful step backward.

Amused and undaunted, Bru turned to Sue. "How about you, Suzie?"

At the wooden image consultant's scandalized negative response, he grinned at Helen, and took her hand in his. "Come on, Helen. You know you want to." Handing his plate to Helen's husband, Hank, he joshed, "Try the calamari, it's not bad. Don't worry, I'll have her home before midnight."

"Mff," Helen's portly husband, Hank, grunted affably,

perking up over the plate of delicacies he suddenly found in his possession.

"Bru," Penelope whispered, blocking his way as he headed toward the dance floor. "Stay here, please. The dancing doesn't usually begin until after the president makes his opening remarks...."

"But after the opening remarks they won't be playing our song," he reasoned, and shot a soulful look at his partner. "Will they, Helen?"

Still slightly stunned, Helen shook her head and shrugged at Penelope.

Jaw slack, eyes wide with horror, Penelope simply stared as her one and only student proceeded to drag the madly blushing Helen onto the empty dance floor.

Tripping the light fantastic wouldn't have begun to describe the scene as Bru whirled Helen into the middle of the floor, putting her through a series of complex swing steps that suddenly had all the mingling practice in the room grinding to a halt. All eyes were on the pair as they maneuvered around the floor to the rousing beat of the music. All eyes, that is, except for Sue and William, who were busy darting scandalized looks in Penelope's direction.

Groping for one of the folding chairs situated against the wall, Penelope sank to her seat in dazed confusion. Dumbfounded, she could only wring her hands and pray for this hideous episode in her career to end. She should have known this would happen. Why hadn't she paid attention to the warning signs? she wondered morosely. Because she'd been more concerned with spending an evening in the company of her exciting client than she had been with his readiness for such an endeavor. She dropped her head into her hands and moaned.

This was all her fault. If she hadn't been so starry-eyed over this corporate cowboy, she might have avoided this disaster. But no. Like a silly schoolgirl in the throes of her first crush, Penelope had overlooked the fact that he was not prepared, and put her own wishes ahead of the client's needs. It was then, with sudden clarity, that Penelope realized that she'd overstepped the bounds of professionalism, and become emotionally involved with a student.

The sound of clapping had Penelope prying her hands away from her eyes and peering through the gathering crowd to the dance floor. People were clapping? She glanced around, surprised. Yes. Clapping to the beat of the music. And smiling. And, by all appearances, having a wonderful time. How could this be? No one was interacting. Making eye contact. Networking. Thunderstruck, Penelope watched in awe as her only student became the veritable life of the party. This wasn't how it worked. Not according to all the courses she'd taken and the books she'd studied.

Helen, eyes sparkling, cheeks flushed, gazed up at her dance partner in amazement. The band smoothly changed gears, and began to play a popular country-and-western ditty. Pulling the nearly swooning Helen close, Bru proceeded to two-step her around the dance floor.

"I'll never hear the end of this," Hank muttered to Penelope as he polished off the last of Bru's appetizers. "She's always ragging on me to take her dancing."

The women in the group began to move closer to the perimeter of the dance floor, chattering excitedly and hoping to be chosen as Bru's next partner. The men, glad to have the pressure taken off, stood back and enjoyed the show. One at a time, Bru danced with different willing and eager partners, exhibiting his dancing prowess as he easily kept pace with any musical curveballs the band tossed his way. He could waltz and foxtrot as easily as he could two-step, and as Penelope worked her way to the edge of the dance floor and stood watching, she valiantly tried to deal with her growing jealousy. Why did every other woman in the place get to dance with him? she wondered, feeling out of sorts. After all, she was the one who had brought him. All around her, the women were salivating over her student.

"Which class is *he* taking?" one woman breathed in awe.

"I don't know, honey, but sign me up!"

The audience howled with delight at Bru's dance moves and several of the previously more staid and sedate women began to scream. Hamming it up, he swiveled around the dance floor. Egging him on, the suddenly rowdy group formed a tight circle around the dance floor and began clapping and gyrating to the beat. Everything that everyone had learned over the past days and weeks flew out the window as Bru moved across the dance floor and plucked Penelope from the crowd.

The last thing Penelope saw before Bru took her in his arms for the most amazing dance of her life was the livid faces of Sue and William. Oh, well, she thought, losing herself in the magic of Bru's embrace. No doubt she'd never get another referral from them. At the moment, she didn't care. Breathless with wonder, Penelope felt almost as if she were skipping on clouds, as Bru whirled her around the floor, pulling her close as the music slowed. Seamlessly he guided her through the foreign steps of a complicated dance, making her feel lithe and graceful and, for once in her life, carefree. She could go on this way forever, she thought dreamily, caught up in the spell that Bru had cast over the entire room.

As the music ended and Bru bent her over backward—his nose nearly touching hers—the crowd roared, and suddenly, Penelope remembered where she was. Her tidy hairstyle was a thing of the past, her pearl barrette dangling, her wavy hair tumbling over her shoulders, trailing on the parquet floor. Struggling to a standing position, she pushed away from Bru, and felt the withering and poisonous looks emanating from William and Sue as they strode over to join them in the center of the dance floor.

Penelope cringed. How had she allowed this to happen?

She wouldn't blame Sue or William for reading her the riot act, right here in front of everyone. And, from the looks of things, that was the plan.

Heading off the eruption, Bru took the offense, both literally and figuratively, with the fuming Sue.

"Hey, Suzie, you're not dancing," he chided at her approach, ignoring her red face. "Care to cut a rug?"

"No." Sue bit the word out, her voice clipped. "I do not dance. In fact, I'm simply appal—"

"Oh. You don't dance. Well. I'm not surprised," Bru drawled, interrupting before she had a chance to blow her cork. "Two left feet? Or—" he grew suddenly solemn "—is it that you are simply so badly out of shape?"

"Ah...ah..." Sue sputtered.

"You know what I think would really fix you up is a big old slab of beef. Being a vegetarian, I know that's probably a turnoff, but I could send you a whole freezerful of some really choice cuts."

"Ah..." Sue gasped.

This was working out better than he'd planned. With a single stone, he was flunking avoiding arguments, admitting he was wrong, exuding friendship and respecting others' opinions—and, if he was really lucky, loud and vexing behavior.

Then why didn't he feel better about it?

It certainly wasn't on account of these two cold fish. Something about them had his hackles rising, and Bru couldn't be sure, but he suspected that professional jealousy had a whole lot more to do with the murderous looks they were shooting at Penelope than the fact that her client had gone off the social deep end. Obviously, Penelope couldn't see what rotten eggs they were. Well, somebody had to save her from herself. Might as well be him.

"You could throw a little barbecue, Suzie. Relax. Crack open a few beers. Because you seem kind of uptight—"

"*Bru,*" Penelope muttered furiously under her breath. "*Please! Your image!*"

"Oh, to hell with my image," he muttered back.

"Would you excuse us for a moment?" Penelope asked and, clutching Bru's sleeve, she proceeded to drag him out of the Grand Ballroom and into a shadowed, relatively quiet corner of the hallway, just outside the giant double doors.

Whirling around, she gripped a fistful of his red satin cummerbund and squinted angrily up at him. "What are you *doing?*" she snapped, valiantly trying to keep her voice down.

"I'm not sure I know what you're talking about."

"You know perfectly well what I'm talking about," she spit furiously, seething with indignation. She couldn't ever remember being this angry. This man could push buttons in her like nobody's business.

"What? They're a couple of dweebs."

"Those dweebs send me a lot of business," she cried. A couple looking for the rest rooms passed by, and Penelope—ever the people-pleaser—smiled at them and called a friendly hello before turning her rabid attention back to Bru. "No wonder Big Daddy wants you to clean up your act! I can't believe the things you said! How arrogant! How insulting! How..." She groped for another word.

Bru took the opportunity to interrupt. "Hey, sometimes the truth hurts."

"Oh, that's rich. This coming from someone who hasn't been honest with me *yet!* You have no intention of ever graduating from my class, do you? No! I can tell from the look on your face. How dare you!" She was shaking now, near tears. "You would let me bring you to this party tonight, knowing full well how important it is to me, and then proceed to make a mockery—"

"Hey, those people back there were having fun—" He suddenly felt rotten to the core. Oh, man. Why hadn't he known hurting her this way would end up scarring him for life?

Slowly shaking her head, Penelope stared at him. "It's almost as if you did all this on purpose. Studied the materials I gave you, looking for a way to…get…to…me…" She gasped, her eyes flashing as she studied his face. "I can't believe it. That's exactly what you did!" Disbelief filled her eyes, her voice. "You don't just want to fail. You want *me* to fail. Don't bother denying it!" she cried, pushing her forefinger into the hard wall of his chest. "I wouldn't believe you anyway. You don't have the guts to tell me the truth."

Snatching her hands away from the front of his shirt, Bru yanked her farther into the secluded corner, away from the curious eyes of the occasional passerby. With a steely grasp, he grabbed hold of her shoulders and hauled her up the long, hard length of his body and angled his mouth within a whisper of hers. His gaze dipped into the fathomless blue sea of her eyes, then dropped to her lips.

"You want the truth?" he rasped, his breathing as ragged as hers. "You want to know how I feel about you and your constant efforts to change me? To turn my life upside down?"

Her answer was a small yelp of surprise, and it was the only sound she made before Bru finally gave in to the urge that had been driving him crazy for what seemed like his entire life. To hell with winning the war with Big Daddy, was his last rational thought. With a frustrated groan, he settled his mouth over hers, kissing her hard, with an intensity that shook them both like an electrical storm. And for the first time in his privileged, powerful life, Bru felt humbled, by a prim little spitfire named Penelope.

Chapter Seven

Penelope felt suddenly bereft as Bru broke their kiss and stared down into her face for a long, tortured moment. It was obvious he was battling something, waging some kind of war deep within himself, the logistics of which she was not privy to. In spite of her frustration with him, she wanted to help. To erase the pensive lines that seemed almost permanently etched into his face. Reaching up, she traced the corners of his mouth and the furrow between his brow, smoothing away those lines with her fingertips. A light sigh escaped her lips.

And that seemed to be his undoing.

With a groan, Bru slid his hands from her shoulders, down her arms and around her waist, as he searched for, and found, her mouth once more. The kiss started out gentle and rapidly grew urgent. Heated. As he pressed her into the wall, Bru deepened their kiss, sending shock waves of delight down Penelope's spine.

Surely this was the moment she'd been waiting for her entire life, she thought hazily, feeling as if she'd suddenly become one with the Fourth of July.

Her relationship with Bru was anything but peaceful, but, she decided as her heart thundered in her ears, as her breathing came in uneven puffs, as her knees turned to oatmeal, though the ride was wild, she had never felt more secure. At this moment, she wouldn't have traded places with another living human being. Yes, life with Bru was like shooting the rapids in a cardboard box, but compared to her heretofore bland, uneventful existence, it was a welcome relief.

To let her emotions out this way was so liberating.

Her eyes fluttered open as Bru's hands roved to her hair, tangling his fingers within the thick tresses.

"I'm a goner," he muttered into her jawline as he kissed her neck, her collarbone, the hollow of her throat.

"Me too," she gasped, and reaching up, ran her own hands through the thick corn silk of his hair. "Oh, Bru," she whispered. "What are we going to do?"

"Well, we're not going back in there, I can tell you that much right now," he said ruefully. "I don't think I'm in any shape to mingle at the moment. Unless," he growled, "it's with you."

Penelope's laugh was deep in her throat. She felt suddenly heady with power. "Stop," she whispered and, at the same time, rolled her head to give him better access to her neck. "We have to go back. We have to get you ready to take over for your father." Actually, she didn't want to think about his father at the moment. And she really didn't want to think about going back into the ballroom. Not with the stubble on his jaw making such a pleasant rasping sensation along the smooth surface of her throat. However, much as she hated talking shop, her time was short. She was caught between a rock that was Big Daddy and a hard place that was Bru.

Drawing his face away from her neck, Bru braced his arm on the wall above her shoulder and looked into her eyes. After a long, heavy expulsion of breath, he groaned.

"Penelope, when will you get it through your wonderful—albeit rock-hard—head that I'm not going back to Brubaker International? My father is nowhere near ready to retire. I'm going to be working the ranch for years!" He tilted her chin with his thumb. "Years, Penelope! But I'm also not going to wait around to inherit my job when I'm a senior citizen. I want to make my own mark on the world. Without waiting for someone else to abdicate the throne." With a heartfelt sigh, he leaned his forehead against hers. "Don't you get it?"

Lolling her face toward her shoulder, Penelope moved her lips to the side of his mouth. "No, Bru!" Her soft words were filled with frustration. "You're the one who doesn't get it!" Lifting her arms, she cradled his cheeks in the palms of her hands and tilted his head back so that she could better look at him. Oh, how she wished Big Daddy hadn't asked her to remain quiet about his thirty-second-anniversary trip. Certainly, that would convince Bru that he needed to finish her class. However, she thought, sighing heavily, Wainrights never broke a confidence.

"Whether you want to or not, you have to finish my classes and get back to your position as CEO." Why was he fighting her this way? She knew he wanted to go back to Brubaker International. He was the only man for the job, and everyone, him included, knew it. So why the protestations? "Why don't you—?"

"Penelope?"

"What?"

"You ask too many questions," Bru muttered, and before she had a chance to finish her argument, he pulled her close for another kiss.

"Oh, for heaven's sake! Would it kill you to just think about go—"

"Save it!" Bru warned in a tightly controlled voice. Exasperated beyond endurance, and more frustrated than he'd ever been in his life, he dragged a hand over his jaw.

Surely, this woman would be the death of him. Perhaps that was Big Daddy's game plan. The last one standing wins.

They hadn't stayed at the party. One realistic look at each other, and they'd had to admit that it wouldn't be kosher to go back into the ballroom looking as if they'd just been wrestling in the hay. Especially considering how livid Sue and William were over Bru's rather politically incorrect remarks. No, that would certainly have been the death knell for Penelope's career.

So they'd summoned the limo and argued all the way back to the ranch. Bru had helped Penelope out of the chauffeured car and up the grand entry to the veranda, where they stood now, continuing the fight that had taken them away from the party in the first place.

"Why are you being so…stubborn?" Penelope cried, dragging her hands through her unruly mane. The pearl clip that held it in its usual tidy style was most likely lying on the floor in some shadowed corner of the hotel. "So…so…" Her voice rose as she groped for the proper description. "…pigheaded?"

Bru rolled his eyes. "Why won't you just give up?" he shot back, his blood really beginning to boil now.

"Because I've been hired to do a job!"

"So quit!"

"Oh, sure. That's your answer for everything, isn't it? Just quit!" She headed for the door.

Grabbing her arm, Bru spun her around, and emitted a sound of fury deep in his throat that suddenly had Penelope quaking in her pumps. Uh-oh. She could tell she'd scored a low blow there, and wished she could pull her foot out of her mouth. He'd had good reasons for leaving Brubaker International, and she knew it.

"Okay, lady," he snarled, rage flying in hot blue sparks from his eyes. "You want me to turn myself into something I'm not? Fine. But before I do, you're going to have to go out on the range with me for a couple of days and count cattle. And—'' his eyes narrowed, stabbing into hers like furious daggers ''—when we are through, if you can tell me when in the blue blazes I'm ever going to use these prissy little manners of yours out there in the middle of nowhere, I'll be happy to finish your damn course.''

"Deal,'' Penelope spit, wondering what on earth she'd just agreed to.

"Good,'' he shot back.

"Fine!'' she shouted.

"Now,'' he ordered, his eyes flashing with passion, "kiss me!''

Sunday mornings in the Brubaker household were always a festive occasion. After a morning trek to church—which took a fleet of luxury sedans just to ferry everyone back and forth—the entire family met for brunch in the formal garden behind the house. Penelope felt privileged to be invited to join the midmorning meal in light of the strict family-only rule that Big Daddy had imposed back when the Brubaker clan was small.

A large brick patio, surrounded by box hedges, rose gardens and various and sundry water fountains and Greek statuary made up the outdoor dining area. A number of side tables, covered in white linen, held silver serving dishes loaded with some of the most spectacular creations Penelope had ever seen or smelled. It almost seemed a shame to eat them. Sunlight streamed through the surrounding live oak and mesquite trees, creating a dappled pattern in this hidden Garden of Eden.

Sunday brunch, Miss Clarise insisted, was the one meal she could count on every week for a little civility. Hence, her brood were still decked out in their Sunday best and exhibiting "good'' behavior.

With a light touch at her back, Miss Clarise lead Penelope to the far end of the table and motioned for her to take a seat across from Bru. "I'm so glad you could be here, darlin','' she said, her cultured voice like a melody.

"With Patsy still in Europe studying dance, it's so nice to have a pretty young girl grace our table."

"Thank you," Penelope murmured, ducking her head. She could feel Bru's gaze, but wasn't brave enough to meet it just yet. Not after the kiss they'd shared at the party last night. And in the limo on the way home. And on the front porch. And, of course, outside her bedroom door. It had taken a great deal of professional fortitude for her to finally push away from the warm comfort of his chest, shake his hand and flee into the safety of her room. She grimaced at her bone-china place setting. What on earth had possessed her to shake his hand? Good grief. No doubt he thought she was some kind of nut. Especially considering how well acquainted she was with his lips. She darted a quick peek at him.

He was staring at her. Smirking. Smiling. Smirkiling, or whatever it was he did with those fantastic lips of his that sent showers of sparks cascading down her spine. Eyes at half-mast, he regarded her sleepily from his place directly across from hers, his dimples growing deeper as the fire in her cheeks did the same.

"Mornin', everyone." Big Daddy's booming voice preceded him as he bounded into the rose garden after having rounded up a half-dozen or so of his younger children. Shooing everyone into their seats, he took his place at the head of the table, his eldest son on one side and his wife on the other. Penelope sat next to Miss Clarise, across from Bru. Mac and Buck took the two chairs at Penelope's left. Once everyone had arrived, and settled into their seats, Big Daddy said grace, then turned to his guest as he tucked his linen napkin into his shirt collar. "Glad you could make it, Penelope, honey. I'm lookin' forward to watchin' Bru's new table mannah's in action." One brow went north, the other south, as the elfin patriarch shot a pointed look at Bru.

Bru grinned rakishly at Penelope.

"Oh, he's been a wonderful student. In fact, many times, I hardly know he's there." Penelope said sweetly.

Mac and Buck guffawed.

"Well, now, that's wonderful," Big Daddy crowed.

The kitchen staff moved silently around the rose garden, pouring water, juice and coffee, serving up plates of delectable gourmet brunch fare and making sure that everyone had simply everything their little hearts desired and more. Penelope had never felt so pampered. Sunday breakfast in the Wainright household generally consisted of Randy's toaster waffles and milk. She wished Randy could see this.

"So," Big Daddy thundered, glancing around the table at his three eldest sons. "What's goin' on around here?"

Carefully listening to their progress reports regarding the running of the cattle ranch, Big Daddy nodded, concurring on some points, disagreeing on others, and—as was usual for him—interfering on most.

Penelope was fascinated by it all.

"What's on the agenda for this week?" Big Daddy thundered his curiosity.

Leaning back in his chair, Bru shot a sidelong look at Penelope as he addressed his father. "Gonna go out and count head in the back sections."

"Good." Big Daddy nodded. "Which ones?"

"All of 'em."

"All of 'em? Why, that'll take the better part of a week!"

Bru grinned lazily at Penelope. "Yep."

"Well, probably not a bad idea. Heard tell that the Bar None and the Double K up the road lost a few hundred head to rustlers over the last couple weeks. Wouldn't hurt us to stop and take some inventory."

Bru frowned. "Rustlers?"

"Yeah," Big Daddy grunted. "Kryson told me yesterday on the golf course. Sons o' guns—pardon my French," he said with a nod to the ladies present, "have been stealing some of the bigger spreads half-blind.'' He sighed noisily. ''Anywho, while you're out there, have a look-see at the fence along the back five or six thousand, take a rough head count and get back to…me…with… Uh-oh.''

Miss Clarise set her teacup down and looked with concern at her husband. ''What is it, darlin'?''

''You can't go out there this week,'' Big Daddy said, slowly shaking his head at his oldest son.

''Why not?'' Bru asked.

''Why not?'' he roared, and, waving a stubby arm, the older man gestured grandly to Penelope. ''You have class, that's why.''

''Yeah, big brother,'' Buck put in, ''you don't want to leave now. Isn't tomorrow handshake day?''

Turning beet red, Mac nearly lost the mouthful of juice he'd just taken as he tried to stifle his laughter.

Bru grinned. ''Well, now, that's not going to be a problem, boy.''

Buck's brow rose. ''No?''

''No.'' Bru shot a blatantly sexy sidelong look at Penelope that had her cheeks suddenly bursting into flames. ''Miss Wainright has agreed to accompany us out on the range, so that I won't have to miss a single minute of my important image education.''

''Wall, now, that's a fine idea!'' Big Daddy beamed back and forth at teacher and pupil. His eyes settled on Penelope. ''But that's a long time for a little lady to be out on the range. Are you sure you're up to it?''

Penelope cleared her throat and blinked down the table at her employer. ''Oh, yes, sir. I'd…uh…love to go out in search of the cattle and, you know, uh, help count them, and at the same time continue instructing my course.''

''You would?'' Mac and Buck were clearly shocked.

''Yes,'' she said, darting a narrow look at Bru. ''It sounds…delightful.''

''Wall, hot diggity dog,'' Big Daddy crowed. ''Etiquette

lessons out on the range. Maybe theah's some hope for these boys yet.''

As he knocked lightly on Penelope's door, Bru had to wonder at his sanity. It was after midnight. Surely she would find his visit a supreme breach in social etiquette. He considered returning to his room before she answered his knock. But it was too late.

''Who is it?'' came her soft query from beyond the door.

''Me.''

Silence.

''Bru.''

''I know. What are you doing here?'' she asked as she opened the door a crack.

He scratched his head. Heck if he knew. He pointed to the bottom of her door. ''I saw the light on under your door and figured you were still up.''

Having spent the day in the company of the entire family, playing lawn croquet, swimming in the pool and visiting with the folks, Bru had not had a moment alone with Penelope since he kissed her good-night last evening. And if he'd thought a cooling-off period would chill his ardor, he'd been wrong. If anything, it had only increased his need to see her. To spend time with her. To…hold her.

Oh, boy, he thought, striding into her room after she opened the door and motioned him inside, he was rapidly losing control of his strategy against Big Daddy.

His contingency plan for the ICAA party hadn't done him a darn bit of good, either. Instead of driving her away, it had merely driven her into his arms. And the ironic part of that whole deal was, she thought his quirky behavior had been her fault. Then, when she found out he'd sabotaged her on purpose, she'd understood. For crying out loud. He couldn't win for losing with this woman.

Well, maybe a week on the range would have her turning her cute little tail and running for the hills. He hoped so. His libido couldn't stand much more of this. Which begged the question, what the devil was he doing in her room after midnight? Was he trying to drive himself insane?

The door clicked shut and, turning, Penelope leaned against it and nervously looked at him. "What can I, uh, do for you?"

Aww, man. He couldn't answer that. At least not truthfully. "I came to see if you were all packed for tomorrow."

"I think so," she said and, pushing away from the door, crossed the room and gestured to the suitcases on her bed.

Bru snorted. "You can't bring all this stuff."

A worried frown marred her brow. "Why not?"

Stepping toward the bed, he began pawing through her suitcases. "Because you don't need most of it," he said with a laugh, and held up one of her colorful scarves. "You can leave these silly scarves and those ridiculous shoes at home."

Penelope took exception to his amused tone. "My wardrobe is neither silly nor ridiculous. These," she snapped, snatching the scarf out of his hand, "are the tools of business."

"Not out on the range, they're not." A slow smile stole across his mouth as he pulled a lacy half-slip out of a silky pile of her lingerie.

Pulling it from between his fingers, she stuffed it back into her case. "Just because a person happens to be out on the range is no reason for one to look unprofessional," she argued, her assertive demeanor flagging somewhat under his amused gaze.

Bru shook his head and snorted.

"Okay! What would you have me take?" she cried, throwing her hands up in defeat.

"Jeans and boots, for starters."

Nudging him out of the way, she began to refold the clothing he'd pulled out of her suitcase. "I don't own a pair of—'' her face wrinkled in disdain as she spat the last word over her shoulder ''—jeans.''

"You can borrow a pair of my sister's." His eyes dropped appreciatively to her derriere. "You look to be about her size. And I'll set out a couple extra pairs of cowboy boots for you to try on. Between Patsy's stuff, and some of my youngest brother's stuff, we'll get you outfitted."

"Well, I guess it wouldn't hurt to take a few extra things," she conceded, "just in case." Turning around, she leaned against the edge of the bed and fingered the fuzzy collar of her robe. Stretching, Bru raised his arms over his head and yawned, and her eyes followed the movements of his muscles beneath his shirt. They were hard muscles. Strong and warm. She knew. Coloring at her wayward thoughts, she forced her eyes away from his body and smiled brightly at her suitcase. "This should be fun."

"Oh, it's a barrel of monkeys," Bru drawled, and took a step toward her. "You'll really have a chance to strut your stuff out there."

"You're insufferable." She grinned in spite of herself.

"I know."

She lifted her gaze to his. "Well."

"Well."

Swallowing, she gestured to the bed. "I should probably finish up. It's getting late."

His eyes shot to the bed, and he nodded. "I'll leave everything outside your door, along with a bedroll and a knapsack. You won't be needing these monsters." Reaching around her waist, he tapped her suitcase.

Time stopped. "Okay," she breathed, wobbling slightly as he bent her over the bed. She clutched his arms for support, and they both straightened.

"I gotta get out of here," he murmured, the look she was beginning to know so well sparking in his eyes.

"Please," she said.

"I'm going." True to his word, he reluctantly dropped

his hand from around her waist and, with a quick, hard kiss on the mouth, moved to the door.

Penelope was suddenly lonely. It was as if he took all the life from the room when he left. "Sweet dreams," she called as he moved into the hallway.

Turning, he looked her up and down and shook his head. "Like hell," he muttered, and disappeared behind the door.

Chapter Eight

"You want to bring the chuck wagon?" Fuzzy scratched his head and, leaning against the rickety wagon, gaped up at his boss. "Bru, we ain't used this old thing since the Summerville Squash Parade, six or eight years ago."

Bru grinned. "I know."

"Chef know you're bringin' the chuck wagon and not the motor home?"

"Chef knows. He's in the kitchen right now, packing enough beans and hardtack and beef jerky and coffee to feed an army.

"Hardtack?" Fuzzy was positively slack-jawed. "Chef?"

"Yes. He's getting a nice Christmas bonus for his...cooperation." With a broad yawn, Bru stretched and brought his coffee cup to his lips. If there was one thing he hated about ranching, it was the early mornings. They were murder on a night owl like himself. Especially this particular morning. Because of one sandy-haired vision in a fussy silk scarf, he hadn't gotten a wink of sleep last night, and it was still several hours before sunup.

"I don't get it," Fuzzy muttered. "And you want to bring the horses." He gestured down the long, wide corridor of stalls from where they stood in front of the main stable's double-doored entry.

"Yep."

"Why? When we have a perfectly good fleet of ATVs?"

Bru's eyes darted to the rugged all-terrain vehicles, parked in the shed near the barn. "I want to get the horses out and work 'em. Besides, like I told you yesterday, the plan is to make her miserable."

"Well, with as little riding as she's done, she'll be miserable, all right," Fuzzy agreed, with a concerned frown.

"Oh, stop worrying. She'll be fine. She's made of pretty sturdy stuff. Why, if I didn't know better, I'd think she was a Brubaker, with that hardheaded stubborn streak of hers. It'll take more than a few days on horseback to get her to admit to Big Daddy that I'm not worth the effort." Admiration tinged his voice. "You packed up the guns?"

"Yep. Ammo, too."

"Thought she'd enjoy some target practice, out away from the cattle in one of the empty sections."

Fuzzy shook his head. "She don't strike me as the type, but—" the grizzled ranch hand shrugged "—I guess that's all part of your plan."

A wide grin split Bru's face. "Yeah. Just part of the plan. So—" leaning against the chuck wagon, he eyed Fuzzy "—who we got comin' on this little trip?"

"Well—" Fuzzy held up his gnarled hand "—there's me and you and Chef and Miz Wainright, that's four. Then there's Mac and Buck and Red. That makes seven."

"What about Jim?" Bru glanced around for the employee everyone jokingly referred to as Grumpy.

"Jim hurt his leg yesterday. Claims he got it caught

between his horse and a fence rail. He's headin' to town today to see the doctor.''

Bru jammed a piece of straw into the corner of his mouth and snorted. ''Man, he's accident-prone. Told me he got that scar on his face opening a bad jar of beans. It's always something with that lazy bag of bones. Ah, well, seven is more than enough. Plus, that'll leave a full crew here for the week, even with Jim laid up for a few days.''

''How long you figure we'll be gone?''

'''Bout a week.''

Fuzzy chuckled. ''Yep. She oughta be longin' for a taste of civilization 'long about Saturday.''

''That's the idea, Fuzzy. That's the whole idea.''

Penelope felt as if her brain might just rattle right out of her head. The jarring gait of the broken-down nag she'd been assigned was enough to churn butter. Burrito. What the heck kind of a name was that for a horse? This was nothing like the thrilling ride she'd taken with Bru. Hanging on for dear life, she nudged the swaybacked animal with her heels, in an effort to find a smoother ride. But it was no use. The bony Burrito had his own pogo-stick rhythm, and as he trotted along, he blissfully ignored the indignant screeches of his rider. Her thighs screamed in agony, her tongue was sore from the half-dozen times she'd managed to bite it, and she was sure that if Bru hadn't packed a chiropractor in the chuck wagon, she would never stand upright again.

The scorching sun was high in the sky now, causing a veritable river of perspiration to trickle steadily between her shoulder blades. Loosening the scarf she wore knotted at her throat, she dabbed at her fiery cheeks with the ends. Surely it was time to stop and eat. To make camp. To enjoy a delicious picnic and perhaps a quick nap, or maybe even a refreshing dip in one of those big pond-type things Bru called tanks. She looked miserably around. How much acreage did Big Daddy have to own, anyway? Certainly the Mexican border, if not the Panama Canal, loomed ahead on the horizon.

They'd been riding for hours over this dusty, lumpy road. Endless, hot, horrible, incredibly uncomfortable hours. The chuck wagon rattled and squeaked, with Fuzzy and Chef bouncing around on top, cackling and shooting streams of tobacco juice into the road, just like something out of a bad spaghetti western. Two cow dogs—Roo-roo and Woof—trotted happily alongside the wagon, seeming not to notice the wretched heat. Fence post after fence post came and went. Here and there, scattered cattle grazed, lifting their heads occasionally to level quizzical stares at the passing circus.

And still they rode.

Thank heaven she'd taken Bru's advice and gone for the jeans. They'd been her one concession to riding gear. Right now, she could probably even have been talked into ripping her shoulder pads out of her summer blazer and stuffing them in her back pockets. Her derriere would never be the same.

After eternity had come and gone, Bru finally rode up beside her, slowing to her pace, sitting his horse as easily as Whistler's mother sat a rocking chair.

"He-he-hello," Penelope rattled, and pushed her bouncing cheeks into a tolerant smile. If she made it off this broken-down crow-bait nag he called a horse in one piece, she was going to smack him.

"Hi." He smiled that sexy, easy cowboy smile that turned her insides to mush. "How's it goin'?"

"F-f-fine."

"Hungry?"

"Ye-ye-yes."

"Good. We should be taking a break here in about an hour or two."

"Wha-wha-what?"

"Yep. Beans and jerky for lunch. Mmmm." He grinned.

Penelope wanted to cry, but she wouldn't give him the satisfaction. "Mmmm," she said and, daring to let go of the saddle horn, patted her tummy. "Mmmm."

The beans were horrible. One bite of the slimy concoction, scraped from the surface of a tin plate, was all Penelope could stomach, she decided once they finally stopped at the side of the road for lunch. For crying out loud. They were still cold. Randy could make a better lunch out of toaster tarts. The jerky was too salty for her taste, and the water and the coffee were both lukewarm.

"Any particular table manners you'd like us to use?" Bru asked politely, handing her a piece of hardtack.

Penelope shot him a withering look through bleary eyes and dropped her hardtack onto her tin plate with a clank. "No table lessons today." Maybe no lessons at all, she thought in exhaustion. Maybe no lessons ever, ever again. "Please—" she waved a tired hand "—suit yourself."

Like a ravenous, lip-smacking eating machine, the six men devoured the beans, jerky and hardtack, washing it all down with cup after cup of the hideous coffee. Several of them belched noisily, and when the dishes—if one could call them that—were cleared away, Chef passed out toothpicks. If she hadn't been so wiped out, Penelope would have been appalled. As it was, she barely had the strength to lean back against the lumpy saddle blanket Bru had tossed on the ground for her comfort. Her eyes slid closed, and she prayed the buzzards would come and carry her off before she had to mount that sorry piece of horseflesh again.

"Well," Bru groaned, hauling himself to his feet, "probably better get back at it. Mac, you ride the fence for a while, check for sags in that low spot that floods in the spring. Red, keep an eye out for cows in trouble. Come on, everyone. We got work to do."

"I don't know 'bout that. Looks like we lost her, boss," Red said, smiling at the slumbering Penelope.

Bru's expression softened as he watched her sleep,

cheeks bright red, hair askew, her scarf and jacket in a tangled heap on the grass beside her. She looked like an angel. "Mac, Buck, come here."

"Huh?" Mac strode over to his brother and grinned down at the sleeping beauty. Behind him, Buck's smiling face peered over Mac's shoulder.

"Tie Burrito to the wagon. I'll take her with me on Lightning." He shook his head, a gentle smile curving his lips as he bent down and lifted her in his arms. She didn't even stir. "Buck, give me a hand mounting up, will ya?"

"Sure, bro."

Buck and Mac exchanged meaningful glances.

For the better part of the afternoon, Penelope, dead to the world, burrowed snugly into Bru's protective embrace.

Limping over to where Bru sat on a fallen log, Penelope paused and, with much painful maneuvering, managed to perch next to him. Oh, she was sore. She felt as if she'd been run over by the chuck wagon. But she wasn't going to let Bru know that. No way. She was here to prove a point. As with a tree falling in the woods, one's image was important even if nobody was around to see or hear it.

And though she would never have admitted it, she was hard-pressed to give a flying fig about her image at the moment. Maybe Bru had been right all along. She had to agree that there didn't seem to be much place for any kind of business protocol out here in the wilderness. Unfortunately, Bru had challenged her to prove otherwise before he would finish her class. Before she could earn her bonus. Well, she had a whole week to give a course here and there. She would bide her time and learn what she could about the ranching business. Look for the right opportunity to illustrate how her skills could come in handy. She glanced dubiously around. Surely they would come in handy.

They'd finally reached the deserted "south-corner" section, where Bru had decided they should make camp. After another despicable supper of beans, hardtack and jerky, washed down with coffee and toothpicks, the men had scattered to do the things they enjoyed most. Red and Fuzzy played noisy games of checkers, Chef stoked the fire and boiled water for dishwashing and general cleanup, and Mac and Buck took care of the horses, fed the dogs, and unloaded bedrolls and other camping gear from the chuck wagon.

"What are you doing?" Penelope asked Bru.

"Polishing my gun." He grinned at her and, despite her multitude of aches and pains, Penelope's heart skipped crazily. Gracious, he was handsome. Especially out here, a rugged man in his element.

"Oh. What do you need a gun for?"

"Target practice, mostly. And the occasional rattlesnake."

Penelope's head snapped up as she scanned the surrounding ground. "Rattler?" She tried to look blasé. Unaffected.

Bru nodded, sighting down the barrel of his gun. "Occasionally. That's why we all wear leg guards from boot to knee."

"Oh." She'd wondered about those.

He patted his gun. "Wanna learn?"

"Me?" she squeaked. "Shoot? Oh, a, ha-ha." Penelope giggled nervously. "I thought I was the teacher here. No, thank you. You go right ahead, though," she said encouragingly.

"You should learn. The way the world's going, it may come in handy someday."

Penelope laughed again, relaxing some. "True, but how would I explain the holster to my students?"

His upper lip curling in his typical style, he grinned broadly at her. "Tell 'em if they don't behave you'll kill 'em."

"Now you tell me." She pretended to pout. "So, that's where I've missed the boat with you. Maybe I should learn to shoot after all.'' Glancing around, she gestured toward the horses, tethered to a patch of live oaks and grazing lazily. ''Won't all that noise scare the horses?''

''Nah. They're used to it.''

''What about the cows?''

''No cattle in this section.'' Standing, he shifted the rifle he'd been polishing under one arm and extended his free hand to her. ''Come on.''

''Where?''

Bru switched his toothpick to the other corner of his mouth and grasped her wrist. ''Over here.''

Tugging her along behind him, he lead her to an area away from the wagon, where he'd set up a series of Chef's empty bean cans on an old, rotting stump. Penelope couldn't think of a more appropriate target.

''Right about here,'' Bru said, coming to a stop and pulling Penelope in close to the front of his body. Pressing his rifle into her hands, he stood behind her, his arms around her body and showed her how to position the wooden stock into her shoulder.

''Like this?'' she asked, her voice unsteady.

''Um-hmm,'' he answered. ''Like that.''

Unbeknownst to them, five pairs of curious eyes had followed them as they moved away from the camp and into the target practice area. And five knowing grins split five masculine faces as Bru slipped his arms around the teacher.

''Old Bru there thinks he's got that little tiger by the tail,'' Fuzzy commented dryly.

''Yep,'' Red agreed with a nod. ''But I'm afeard it's got him.''

''Why do you call him Roo-roo?'' Penelope asked Bru as she pointed out one of the two cow dogs that had accompanied them on this trip. It was the morning of day two, after another deplorable breakfast of beans, hardtack and coffee, and a sponge bath out of a canteen that had left Penelope feeling anything but revitalized. The sun was just beginning to peep over the eastern horizon, sending the first rays of morning softly into their camp area. Birds chattered in a neighboring tree as they prepared to ride to the first of over a dozen sections to count cattle.

Reaching down, Bru patted the dog's silky head. "Because that's what he wants to be called."

Penelope smiled skeptically. "How do you know that?"

"Well—" Bru paused and scratched his chin "—when he was just a pup, I asked him what his name was, and he said, 'Rrroo-oo-oo-roooo!'"

Laughing, Penelope planted her hands on her hips. "So that's why you call the other one Woof?"

"Yep. That, and the fact that he thinks he's a wolf." Ambling over next to her, Bru put his hands on her shoulders and murmured in her ear. "Don't tell him he's not. It would hurt his feelings."

"Okay," she whispered, and shivered as his warm breath caressed the hair at the side of her neck, "your secret is safe with me."

"Let's count some cattle," Mac called, interrupting their private moment as he swung up onto his mount.

"Guess that means us," Bru said apologetically, and before Penelope knew what hit her, she was back in the saddle, trying to keep her teeth from rattling out of her head.

"Twenty six hundred and fifty," Bru shouted to Mac over the noisy bellowing of the cattle. Dust, churned by thousands of pounding hooves, filled the air.

"Fifteen?" Mac shouted back.

Bru shook his head. "Fifty!"

Mac nodded and jotted the figure down in a small notebook and, stuffing it into his pocket, rode around the holding pen where they'd been counting the cattle in the south middle section that morning. Reining in his mount, Mac pulled up next to Penelope, where she sat on Burrito's back, watching in fascination.

"How you doin'?" he queried pleasantly.

"Hi, Mac. How does he know how many are there?" she asked, not quite believing what she had seen. Only minutes before, Bru had come galloping up to the holding pen, squinted at the herd for a moment and called the number to his brother. It was the third time she'd seen him do it that morning. "He didn't even count them. Is he just guessing, or what?"

"Oh, no, ma'am. If there were twenty six hundred and fifty-one, he'd have told me."

"No!" Penelope cried, eyeing him skeptically. "You're pulling my leg."

Mac grinned. "Well, if he's off, it's only by one, plus or minus. If you don't believe me, count 'em yourself. I'd bet my next paycheck he's right."

Her eyes swung to Bru as he whistled for his dogs, commanding them to chase down a stray calf. "Go get 'em, Woof. Left. Bring 'em in. Let's go, Roo. Good boy." A signal to his horse turned him around, and he cantered over to where Fuzzy and Red sat on their mounts and issued a few instructions.

The sun bathed him in a sepia-toned glow as he threw back his head and laughed at something one of his men said. Leaning forward in his saddle, he shouted a response that had them all nodding together. Then, as if he could feel her watching him, he lifted his eyes and his gaze caught hers in that explosive connection that was becoming so familiar to them both. A slow smile stole across his mouth, and he nodded at her. Once again, she was swept across the sea of cattle, through the billows of dust and into the bottomless vortex of his gaze. Heart pounding, blotting out the sound of the animals lowing, Penelope suddenly had the feeling that she'd stepped into a time machine and been zapped back a hundred and fifty years, to an era when the men were men and the women were...impressed.

As the first few days out on the range passed, Penelope learned more about life on a large, working cattle ranch than she had ever dreamed there was to learn. And if she'd ever been impressed by a firm handshake, effective speech or steady eye contact, it paled to nothingness compared to the way Bru and his men could do the work of a small army and make it look easy.

The very fact that they didn't seem to mind existing on cold beans and tasteless hardtack was enough for them to deserve to be awarded the Congressional Medal of Honor, in her opinion. For the past two nights, they'd all slept on the hard, lumpy ground out under the stars, in bedrolls near the fire, then woken the next morning before daybreak, to start yet another arduous workday. She had yet to hear anyone complain. About anything.

She, on the other hand, felt as if she'd aged a hundred years, at least. Stiff and achy from her uneasy rest on her makeshift bed, sleepless from listening to the sonorous breathing of six slumbering men, irritable and ravenous from the lack of a decent meal, and bruised and sore from Burrito's ungodly gait, she wanted to scream. Her hair felt as if it harbored at least an acre of Big Daddy's land, so dry and gritty was it to the touch. No amount of conditioner would ever repair the damage, she was sure. And, even though she'd brought plenty of clean clothes, and there was more than enough water for the occasional spit bath and shampoo job, she still felt gritty and rumpled. The colorful scarf knotted at her throat did nothing to make her feel the consummate professional she'd heretofore known herself to be.

But, in spite of the physical discomforts, Penelope was having a remarkably good time. Just living out in the wide-open spaces, with none of the pressures of the modern world to intrude, was so incredibly liberating. She had never known such freedom, and had even taken to leaving off her jacket and rolling up her sleeves now and again. There was always something interesting going on, and the men were all so nice to her, treating her as part of the gang, even though she had yet to get up on Burrito's back without Bru's grinning help.

From a business standpoint, the trip was moderately successful, as she'd even managed to impart a lesson or two along the way. Generally, after a meal, one of the men— never Bru—would ask her a business-related question.

"No kiddin'," Fuzzy had exclaimed after dinner that evening, as they all sat reclining around the campfire learning about the wonderful world of image enhancement. "You mean to tell me, if I commit my goals to paper, it's the first step in my journey to achievement?" He shook his grizzled head in disbelief.

"Yes." Penelope beamed. "Try it. You'll be amazed at the results."

"Wall, don't that beat all!" Red breathed, clearly fascinated by the tricks of her trade. "Say, now, Miz Wainright, would you mind going over that part about them seven surefire ways to make people like you?" Red grew ruddier as bashful heat rushed up his neck and into his face, like the mercury in a thermometer.

"Of course, Red," Penelope said, reaching into her satchel and pulling out a course file. "Although I think you have a pretty good idea about that already."

Beaming, Red lived up to his name.

Handing him a handout, she explained, "Everything you need to know is all right here. Study these tips, put the basic principles into action, and see what happens."

Chef leaned forward. "Toss me one of those, will you, honey?"

"Sure."

"Me too," Mac said, taking one and distributing the others.

Penelope smiled broadly at their animated faces, thrilled

with their interest. If only she could get her paying student to show as much desire to learn. Her eyes strayed to where Bru sat, several yards away, leaning against his bedroll, apart from the group, patting Roo and Woof and watching her lazily from beneath the brim of his hat. Her eyes locked with his, and her blood began to heat as she attempted to continue her lesson.

"I guarantee these, uh, seven tips in interpersonal communication will have friends and, um, colleagues alike seeing things your way. It's—" she touched her lips with her tongue "—uh, far easier to catch er, uh, flies with honey…"

Slowly, Bru's eyes forked at the corners, as the smile that threatened his mouth finally came out of hiding. Penelope swallowed. The things that man could do to her heart rate without even touching her. She blinked and tried to look away, but couldn't.

She forged ahead, despite the dizziness that assailed her. "…ah, than it is with…uh, vinegar," she stammered, still unable to tear her gaze from the dark and mesmerizing eyes that seared her with their intensity.

"True," Fuzzy nodded and stroked his beard. "Never thought of it that way."

Trying to seem unflappable, she laughed. "Okay, then," she said, noting—much to her chagrin—that her laughter was breathless. "Uh, I guess that would conclude this evening's lesson."

"Thank you, Miz Wainright," Red said reverently, clutching his notes in his callused hands and pressing them to his chest. "I'll study up, and have some questions fer ya tomorrow."

"I look forward to that, Red."

"I'll quiz ya in the mornin' on the way over to the west section," Fuzzy told him, taking his harmonica out of his shirt pocket and banging it on his thigh.

Penelope smiled and reloaded her satchel with books and class materials as the impromptu class broke up and the men scattered to perform the nightly rituals that needed doing before bed. Striking up a soulful cowboy tune, Fuzzy settled in by the fire to entertain the troops.

Bru—unbeknownst to Penelope—had instructed that all radios and CD players be left at home this trip. Though it did not escape him that she didn't seem to miss the luxury of stereo sound out here in the middle of nowhere. It seemed he was doomed to be thwarted at every turn by her chipper resolve to reform him. No matter how miserable he tried to make her life, she had a way of bouncing back. Of taking life's problems and turning them into challenges. Of taking life's lemons and making a blasted lemon meringue pie.

He hated that about her.

He loved that about her.

There was a slight chill in the air, Bru noted, absently scratching one of the dogs between the ears. It would be a little colder than usual tonight. Probably should rustle up another blanket for Penelope. Luckily, they'd been camping near a grove of live oaks. Thick as they were, if the weather got wet, they would afford some protection from the elements. Wouldn't hurt to bank the fire some, too, he thought, and with a groan he hauled himself to his feet.

Bru walked over to stand behind Penelope. "Looks like it might rain."

She gasped, as if he'd startled her, then turned her head to look at him. "Really?" Penelope pushed her satchel out of the way to make room for him to sit down next to her.

Once the fire was burning brightly, he lowered his frame to the ground and leaned back against the blankets Penelope had rolled and stacked for their makeshift dinette set. The guys had loved them, claiming the beans never tasted better than when eaten on these comfortable seats.

"Oh, it won't start yet." He sighed, settling back and tilting his head to look at her. "Maybe tomorrow."

Lifting her gaze, Penelope stared thoughtfully at the

gold and orange streaks on the horizon. "How can you tell?"

"I don't know." He shrugged. "I just can."

She smiled. "You can do a lot of things."

"You too."

"No." Pink spots appeared on her cheeks. "Not like you. You can do anything. And you do it well. For example, how did you learn to dance so well?"

Bru snorted. "It wasn't my idea, I can tell you that much."

"No?" Penelope was surprised. "Did your father make you learn?" There was a certain amount of sympathy in her voice.

"No. My sister. Patsy's the dancer in the family. When we were kids growing up, it seemed like every time I turned around, she was nagging me to practice with her. Since all my other brothers were... What's the word I'm looking for?" he wondered aloud, raising his voice and shooting an amused glance at his brothers, where they'd settled by the fire and begun a game of cards.

"Say what?" Buck wondered, shifting his attention and peering over his cards at his eldest brother.

"Klutzes." Bru nodded sagely at Penelope. "That's the word I'm looking for."

"Hey," Mac drawled, tossing a card on the discard pile, "we were just smart enough not to get caught in sis's ballet web, that's all."

Eyes twinkling, Bru looked conspiratorially over at Penelope. "Nah," he murmured under his breath. "Klutzes." He mouthed this word and pointed at his brothers.

Penelope grinned. She loved the easy feeling of camaraderie they'd all slipped into. Like family. Shooting a peek at Bru's handsome face, she felt her heart skip a beat. Well, not exactly like family, she amended to herself.

"Anyway, when Patsy wants something, Patsy gets it. It was easier just to give in than to fight Patsy. She's determined. A lot like my mother.'' Bru shifted his gaze, angling his head toward Penelope. "A lot like you, actually.''

"Oh?''

"That's a compliment.''

Flustered, Penelope changed the subject, encouraging him to spin more tales of his youth. Now and again, his brothers would join in on the storytelling, and regale her with some of the more comical episodes having to do with life in the Brubaker household. Penelope would find herself holding her sides, tears of laughter streaming down her face, begging them to stop before she exploded. With Fuzzy playing soulfully in the background, and three handsome brothers to entertain her, Penelope couldn't think of another more wonderful place on the face of this earth that she'd rather be. Slowly, the sun drifted down to tickle the western horizon and then, in a wild bouquet of color, sank out of sight.

Engrossed in conversation, Bru and Penelope barely noticed how late it was getting. As darkness overtook them, one by one, the men slipped into their bedrolls. From the other side of the fire, Chef began to serenade them with his deep and often thunderous breathing.

"Man, I hope I don't sound like that,'' Bru said, chuckling at the buzz saw that emanated from Chef's bedroll.

"You don't.''

Twisting, Bru arched a teasing brow and eyed her suspiciously. "How do you know?''

Penelope rolled her eyes. "Oh, don't go and get a swelled head. I wasn't laying there, studying your breathing patterns.'' At least not all night long, she thought with a smile. "I'm a light sleeper, so this…cacophony, if you will, keeps me awake sometimes. Seriously, I can close my eyes and tell you who is snoring.''

"No way.''

"Yes,'' she boasted.

"Now that's talent.'' Bru ruffled her hair playfully, and

suddenly it was as if the rest of the world fell away. After a long moment, Bru raised his thumb and stroked her cheek. "We should probably go to bed."

"Yes." The word was shaky. Barely a whisper.

"It's late."

"Yeah," she breathed.

"We have to get up early."

"Uh-huh." Racking her brain, Penelope searched for a reason to prolong their conversation. Sitting up a little straighter, she looked up at him. "Uh, Bru?"

"Yeah?"

"I was wondering if we could have some target practice tomorrow night after dinner?"

His jaw dropped, and he stared at her for a long time, slowly shaking his head.

"Unless, uh…" she said, and shrugged, "you don't, you know…want to."

Reaching for the back of his neck, he rubbed the muscles there and smiled, as if at some private joke. "No, that would be fine." Gathering his lanky legs beneath him, he stood and extended his hand to her. When she was upright, he stood looking at her and continued to hold her hand in his. Again he slowly shook his head. "In fact, I was going to ask you."

"Really?" she breathed, pleased. "Okay, then. Well… good night."

"Good night," he murmured, squeezing her hand in his.

A noisy, disgusted sigh came from the other side of the fire, near Chef. "Ain'tcha gonna kiss her?" Fuzzy demanded in a stage whisper that could have been heard back at the main house.

Mac and Buck and Red guffawed from beneath the blankets of their bedrolls, rolling and punching each other like so many boys at summer camp. Only Chef slept on, a lone chain saw in the rhythm section of the dreamland express.

Bru was obviously taken aback, his eyes widening in surprise.

Feeling her cheeks leap with flames brighter than their campfire, Penelope cast her eyes quickly about, looking for an escape route. A way to let Bru off the hook in front of his men. She could pretend she simply had not heard Fuzzy, she thought wildly, pulling her hand from his grasp and wringing them together in mortification. Unable to stop herself, she lifted her eyes to Bru's, and what she saw there took her breath away.

"You heard the man," he whispered and, taking a step toward her, pulled her hands back into his.

"No, I, uh..."

"I'm supposed to kiss you good-night."

"Me?" she squeaked.

"Well, I'm not kissing him, if that's what you're askin'." He grinned.

Penelope giggled at the image. "No," she whispered, glancing over at the audience of three lying in the shadows. Leaning on their elbows, they were making no bones about the way they were grinning and staring at the pair who stood by the fire. She giggled again, feeling incredibly self-conscious. "Okay, then," she said, angling her cheek up toward Bru's mouth.

Whistles and catcalls came from the flickering shadows of the peanut gallery. Chef snorted and turned over.

Grinning, Bru grabbed Penelope's hand and lead her into the darkened area behind the chuck wagon.

"Hey," Fuzzy called in protest. "Where ya goin'?"

"I'm kissing the lady good-night," Bru returned, leaning against the wagon and pulling Penelope into his arms. "So go to sleep, gentlemen."

A chorus of moans and groans drifted through the night air, mingling with the cricket's song and fading into so much background noise. With a heavy groan of his own, Bru cupped Penelope's face in his hands and, using the moonlight as his guide, sought and finally found her mouth with his.

And before Bru had finished kissing the starch out of

his starchy image teacher, the peanut gallery had joined
the trumpet section of the dreamland express.

"Stop, Penelope."

Penelope paused as Bru's voice—deadly calm—came
from over her shoulder. It was after dinner the following
evening, and they'd been shooting in the practice area,
moving from stump to stump, knocking off a series of bean
cans as they went. Though she had a lot to learn, Penelope
was having a ball. Who knew target practice could be so
fun?

"Don't move."

"Is this a stickup?" She giggled. "Well, I'm not carrying anything of value. Unless—" she angled her head
thoughtfully "—you count my virtue." Again, she
laughed.

Bru snorted impatiently. "I want you to stand perfectly
still, and don't even look at me."

"Why not?" Rolling her eyes, she grinned and planted
her hands on her hips. Before he ordered her to stop, she
had been on her way to the stumps in the target practice
area to reset the cans. "Are you afraid I'll set all my cans
on the easy stump?" she called saucily over her shoulder.
All evening, he'd been pouting and pretending to be mad
about the fact that she'd beaten him in round one of flip-
the-can. But she knew he wasn't really mad. After all, it
had been a lucky shot for her. Normally, he beat the socks
off her, even with his eyes closed.

And she still hadn't gotten the hang of loading her gun.
Of course, that didn't surprise her. Most machines were
beyond her ability to operate. Penelope was a people person. Relationships were her forte.

"So," she asked, breezily, flipping her loose hair over
her shoulder. Some cow or another had trampled her barrette a day or two ago. "Would you mind telling me
what's going on?"

"Dammit, Penelope, will you shut up with the questions for once?"

Tttsssssssszzzzzz...

A riot of gooseflesh suddenly sambaed down Penelope's spine. She'd heard that sound before. Once. On the Discovery Channel.

"Bru?" she asked in a tiny, squeaky voice.

Suddenly her knees went weak. Her heart slammed violently against her ribs, threatening to burst out of her chest. She was going to faint. She was afraid to look. Squeezing her eyes tightly shut, she listened. It sounded close. As close as the stump she'd been on the verge of reaching. Face scrunched into a wad of fear, she chanced a peek through her lashes. It was... It was!

"Sssssnaaakke," she whimpered, beginning to quake in earnest.

It was true. For there—rattles rattling, head swaying, eyes cold and calculating—coiled in a menacing pose on the far target stump, not more than five or six feet from where she stood, sat a snake. And he didn't exactly look pleased with the ruckus Bru and Penelope had been kicking up.

"Easy now, sweetheart," Bru murmured. Behind her, she heard a soft click. Bru had cocked his gun. He took aim. "Don't move an inch," he instructed. Another click. Several choice swear words. "Empty." Several more pithy expletives.

Oh, why hadn't she learned to load her gun?

Tttsssssssszzzzzz...

Yes, she was definitely going to faint. "Hurry," she sang through tightly clenched teeth. "Hurrrrrrrrry." Again she whimpered, mewling sounds born of terror escaped her throat. "Bruuuuuuuuu."

"Hold still," he instructed, as he crouched low to the ground.

Suddenly a whizzing, coming from behind her this time,

as something flew past her shoulder, through the air. A thwack, and then...silence.

"He's history." Bru sighed, righting himself and striding over to the stump to check out the two separate pieces of what had been a rattlesnake.

"Oh, B-B-Bruuu," Penelope wailed, dropping to her knees, shaking like a leaf. "Oh, my word, oh my word, ohmyword," she babbled, and buried her face in her hands.

Running to her side, Bru dropped down beside her and took her in his arms. "Hey, sweetheart, it's okay now," he said, bringing his face next to hers and stroking her hair. "He can't hurt you. Look, see? He's dead. Oh, honey, don't cry. Hey, hey, hey," he crooned, his tone soothing and gentle, as he brushed at her tears with his hands and rocked her back and forth.

She settled on his lap, clutching his shirt in her fists, and sobbed into his neck, releasing her terror in great, heaving breaths.

"Oh, Bru, I was so...so...sca-sca-scared," she stammered, rubbing her watery face against his flannel-covered shoulder.

"I know, me too, honey."

"No! You weren't! You were brave!" Eyes watery, she blinked up at him. "I was petrified. I can't believe you did that. I can't believe you killed a snake with a rock."

Bru grinned. "I had to. You forgot to load your gun."

"How'd you know that you could do that? I mean, what if you missed?"

"I've had to kill a snake or two before. Learned that particular method from Big Daddy. One time, he and my mother were driving along, and he skidded to a stop, hopped out of his rig and, picking up a flat stone, cut the head right off the biggest rattler you've ever seen. Impressed the heck out of Mom. He cut the rattles off and gave 'em to her. She treasures them more than her wedding rings, I think."

The sound of Bru's voice as it rumbled in his chest was soothing. Lifting her head away from the comforting resonance, she peered up at him through watery eyes. "See. You can learn a thing or two from your father," she murmured, and shot him a wobbly grin.

Tracing the curve of her lips with his fingertips, Bru returned her grin. "Yep. You got a point there. We all practiced skipping stones, hoping to someday be as good as Big Daddy. Keeps us from getting bored. I told you we get the occasional snake out here."

Penelope ventured a fearful peek over Bru's shoulder, her arms still locked tightly around his neck. "How occasional?"

"Hey, now," Bru chuckled. "Don't worry. Stick by me, and you'll be fine."

"Oh—" Penelope sighed, burrowing farther into his embrace "—I'm not going anywhere."

Chapter Nine

"It's raining," Bru called. The sarcasm in his voice was negated by his grin as he trotted up to where Penelope had been sitting and waiting out the shower.

"What was your first clue?" Penelope asked as raindrops trickled over the yellow plastic rain hat she'd been given and plopped off the end of her nose. Water sprayed everywhere as she shook her head. "Sorry, Burrito," she muttered to her mangy mount, and patted the bones that stuck sharply out at his neck. Clutching the slippery saddle horn, she twisted in her seat and looked up as Bru approached on Lightning. She was incredibly relieved to see him. It was getting downright chilly out here. "So. It would seem you were right about the rain."

"I thought you understood by now that I'm always right," he said, teasing.

She snorted, and guffawed rudely. Gracious. A week out on the range, and she was acting just like one of the guys.

"What are you doing out here, all by your lonesome? I thought you promised to stay close." Pulling up next to her, he leaned forward in his saddle and displayed his dimples to her. Covered from head to toe in a yellow plastic poncho, he looked relatively dry and comfortable.

Penelope, on the other hand, felt like a cornflake that had been sitting in milk all day. Luckily, that morning she'd thought to loop several of her colorful scarves around her neck. They were coming in very handy as towels at the moment. And Bru said dressing for success out on the range was a waste of time. Ha!

"Oh, that." Droplets flew as she waved an airy hand. "That was back in the olden days, when I thought I might get bit by a snake." Smiling, she brushed the water out of her eyes to better see him. "When I started to drown, though, I decided to head for higher ground." She shrugged. "Trouble is, there is no higher ground." Pointing to a grove of live oaks not far away, she said, "It's dry under those trees. Maybe we should all head over there." The rain had finally began to seep through her clothes, causing gooseflesh to shiver up her spine.

"No, I sent everyone back to camp. The ground is higher in the camp section. That's why I came over here to get you. We're calling it a day. It's raining too… hard…to…get…anything… *Man!*"

The clouds opened up as he was speaking and let forth a deluge the likes of which Penelope had never seen. Blinking rapidly, she ducked her head and watched the water sluice off the brim of her hat in a solid, unending sheet. Poor Burrito, she thought, patting the trusty, albeit soggy, animal. He didn't even have a hat. She murmured soothing phrases to the horse that had his ears twitching as he listened.

From his perch high up on Lightning's back, Bru looked around, the expression on his face grim. "I don't like this," he muttered.

"What?" Penelope shouted, straining to hear him over the sudden squall.

Raising his voice, he turned to face her. "I don't like the way it's been raining so hard all day, like this. The ground is too dry. Can't soak it all up. This area floods sometimes.'' Gesturing with his arm, he pointed out the gully that dipped beneath the section of fence Mac had spent the morning checking.

Even as they stood there, the rain began to puddle on the ground. With remarkable speed, the puddles grew, reflecting the charcoal color of the sky.

"Come on!" Bru shouted, even though he was sitting right next to Penelope. "Let's get under those trees. When it lets up some, we can head back to camp."

"Okay." Nodding, Penelope urged Burrito to follow him to the stand of live oaks. At least Bru had a poncho to keep him dry. She'd opted to leave hers back at the house, bringing only her hat for protection. But how was she supposed to know that a rainstorm—the magnitude of which would probably have had Noah running for his hammer and saw—would soak her to the skin before the end of the week? It was summertime, for crying in the night. In Texas, of all places.

Once they made it to the trees, Bru found a dry spot for them under the leafy foliage, and beckoned for her to join him. They stayed mounted on their horses, and sat next to each other, watching in awe as the water poured out of the sky.

"I bet it doesn't rain this hard in a tropical rain forest," Penelope breathed.

"Flash flood weather," Bru muttered.

She shivered. "No. R-r-really?"

"Seen it happen." He shrugged.

She shivered again. This time, although she tried, she couldn't seem to stop. Her teeth began to clack in a most annoying fashion—whether from nerves or the dampness, she couldn't be sure.

"Hey." Turning in his seat, he leaned forward and peered at her, concern etched in the furrow between his eyes. "You're shivering. And no wonder." He reached over and felt her light summer jacket. "You're soaked. To the skin!'' He began to unfasten his poncho. ''Here, take this and put it on.''

''N-n-no, no, no,'' Penelope said through her chattering teeth. ''Don't be silly. You need that.''

Bru shook his head, his expression brooking no argument. ''Penelope, don't give me any grief, okay? Just put it on.''

''O-k-k-kay.'' The poncho harbored the wonderful remnants of Bru's body warmth, and as it began to radiate into her cool and clammy flesh, she shivered all over again. Violently. Her neck and jaw ached from the uncontrollable spasms.

Taking her hand in his, Bru rubbed it vigorously, and blew his warm breath on her fingers. ''We need to get you back to camp. You need a hot cup of coffee,'' he stated flatly, his eyes filled with concern.

''Just don't make me eat any b-b-beans.'' She'd rather die in a flash flood. ''I'll be fine in a m-minute. Honest,'' Penelope said with a determined smile, trying to show that she could take it. She had to show him that she was as tough as the next guy when it came to working the ranch. That way, Bru wouldn't have an excuse not to give his all to her class next week, when they were back at home. Lifting her wrist, she dabbed at her nose, to see if it was still there. Ohhhhh... She was miserable, and if she didn't know better, she would have sworn that even Burrito was shivering.

''I don't believe you. You don't look fine to me.''

''Oh, you sweet-talker,'' Penelope gasped, and sniffed and pushed some wet strands of hair away from her eyes. ''You know what I mean.''

As he took her hands and pressed them to his face, Penelope could feel his cheeks lift in a smile beneath her fingertips. His gaze strayed to the rising puddles, and his smile faded as he watched them begin to connect and flow into the gully. Bru shook his head. ''That does it. We can't stay here. It's not safe. I don't want to get caught in a flash flood, and we have to get you out of the rain. But I don't want to risk riding across the gully to camp." He exhaled slowly, thinking.

"I'm sorry," Penelope whispered. "I never should have ridden so far away from the group b-by myself."

"Don't be ridiculous. I should be the one apologizing. I never should have let you get out of the house without some rain gear."

"Ah. N-n-next time. If there is a next time." Her laughter came in hiccups. "I'd kill for a hot b-bath."

"Too bad the house is so far away… Wait a second.…" Rubbing his jaw, Bru looked toward the horizon as inspiration struck. "Let's go."

"Where?" Penelope asked.

"We've got a little supply cabin, up ahead several miles. Fence crew uses it from time to time. It's up on a knoll. If we hurry, we can make it in about half an hour."

"Half an hour?"

"It's better than sitting here, waiting for someone to send a life raft."

"Is it that bad, Bru?"

He looked at her for a worried moment before replying. "It's not good."

It took nearly an hour to pick through the deep pools of standing water and finally make it to the cabin. Midway there, Burrito was spooked by a particularly loud clap of thunder, and Penelope was afraid he might try to run away with her. So she joined Bru on Lightning's back and they rode the second half of the journey together. Burrito followed docilely along, once the thunder died down.

Penelope was glad to be riding with Bru for more reasons that she cared to contemplate. The ride was obviously much smoother, and he was very good at fording the more intimidating puddle-ponds. Plus, his body warmth helped to still her shivers.

But if Penelope was brutally honest with herself, the

reason she most wanted to ride with Bru was the fact that she hated every second she spent away from his presence. This crushing reality had dawned on her that afternoon, as she rode alone, looking for a dry place to rest. How depressing. All her life, she'd fancied herself a reasonably happy person. Content. Well-adjusted. Unfortunately, the very thought of going back to that happy, content, well-adjusted life struck terror in her heart.

How could she survive without Bru?

She would have to learn, she guessed. Once the lessons were over, she'd have to go back to her mundane nine-to-five life at the office. The idea was utterly bleak. No wonder Bru loved it out here so much. It was so exhilarating. So full of life. So full of...love.

She frowned. Most likely all those things were because of the man who was currently holding her so securely in his embrace. If it wasn't for him, would she find this life so enchanting? Glancing around at the endless acres that were rapidly becoming a sea, she decided she probably wouldn't. The romance of this place came from the way this man looked at it.

Nestling back against his chest, she pressed her ear to his shirt and listened to the steady murmur of his heart and wished dispiritedly that she had a place there. Unfortunately, she had a feeling that his heart was already filled to bursting with this ranch. There would be no room there for Brubaker International, let alone an image consultant who hadn't yet learned how to let her hair down and live a little.

Penelope sighed heavily. How ironic that she should find true love so far away from the business world. Well, she would have to get over it. The man who fell in love with her would have to be able to accept her just the way she was. He would have to share her interest in business. He would have to put up with her stubborn streak. And he'd have to accept her little family. It was a lot to ask.

Most likely, a renegade like Bru was not up to the task. Certainly he didn't want to be.

Again she exhaled heavily, and tightened her grip on the arms that circled her waist.

"How you doin'?" he murmured, bringing his warm lips close to her ear.

"Fine." She turned her head and leaned back against his mouth. "I'm finally starting to warm up now. So...thanks."

"My pleasure."

"Mine too," she blurted out, before she could stop herself. She could feel his smile against the side of her head. Her heart raced.

"We're almost there." Tightening his grip, he pulled her more closely into the wall of his body. "You'll be able to see the cabin off in the distance, just over this next rise."

Too bad, she thought sadly. She could stay like this forever. Without the rain, of course. "You know," she said conversationally, "I've had a good time this week."

Bru threw back his head and laughed.

Pushing against him, Penelope tucked her chin to her shoulder and peeked back up at him. "What's so funny?"

"Oh, nothing." Shaking his head, he hauled her back against his chest. "You. Me. Everything. I have a secret."

"Oh, yeah?"

"Um-hmm. I had a great time, too. Best ever, actually."

Shivers—this time of delight—tingled and skipped throughout her body. Best ever. Why? Couldn't be because of the image lessons. Or the snake. Or the rain. Or the lumpy nights on the ground. She didn't care. Just hearing him say that he'd enjoyed having her along made everything worthwhile.

"Next time, though," he mused, "you're bringing some decent clothes."

Next time? She grinned from head to toe. There would be a next time? Really? Why? When? She was just screwing up her nerve to question him on the subject when the cabin came into view.

"There she is," Bru murmured, pointing to a beautiful dwelling that would have looked quite normal gracing a cul-de-sac in most upper-middle-class neighborhoods. "There's the cabin."

"Cabin?" Penelope frowned. If that was a cabin, what in heaven's name would he call her apartment? "The lights are on. Did you call ahead and arrange for a staff to serve us?" she quipped, eager to get out of the rain, and hopefully find something—anything that wasn't beans—to eat.

"No," Bru sounded puzzled. "That's odd."

"What's odd?"

"Looks like somebody's already here."

Chapter Ten

"Who do you think is here?"

Bru frowned and, giving the reins a slight tug, slowed Lightning's gait. "One of our ranch hands. You've met him. The guy with the scar on his cheek."

"Jim?"

Bru nodded. "Kind of a bellyacher. He's supposed to be laid up with a bum leg. Wonder what he's doing out here?"

"How can you tell he's here?" Penelope looked at the deserted cabin, bewildered.

"That's his rig, parked next to that cattle truck on the other side of the cabin."

Bru shook his head in disgust. He'd told those chowderheads to stay back at the stables and take care of business while he was gone. Criminy. Couldn't those guys follow a simple order for once? What the heck were they thinking, bringing the cattle truck—full of cattle—clear out here in this weather? And who had authorized them to buy more cattle in the first place? Had Big Daddy gotten some kind of deal?

Bru snorted. Now, they probably wouldn't be able to drive back until tomorrow, the way the water was standing on the back access roads. He couldn't leave those clowns for five minutes without all hell breaking loose.

There went his little fantasy of spending time all alone with Penelope this afternoon. Now he'd have his crew hanging around, eavesdropping on everything and yucking it up. Grinding his teeth in frustration, he guided his horse around the opposite side of the house and headed for a dense grove of trees.

"Listen, honey, would you mind staying out here under these trees with the horses for a few minutes?" Leaning forward, he peered into her face and smiled apologetically. "I need to go in there and talk to my men about following orders. I'll come and get you when I'm done kicking some butt. Okay?"

"Okay," she whispered.

Penelope angled her face back up to his and smiled, the rain sparkling on her lips. Unable to resist the temptation, Bru reached to her mouth and traced the pattern of drops with the pad of his thumb.

"I won't be long."

"Good." The word, breathy and warm, tickled his fingers. Bru stared at her. That did it. Jim and whoever else were all walking back. Swimming, if they had to. He couldn't wait to get rid of those idiots and have Penelope all to himself. Images of the two of them, cuddled together in front of the fire, began to heat his blood.

"And, Bru?"

Man. When she looked at him like that, he couldn't think straight. "Yeah?"

"Remember, you can always catch more flies wi—"

"With honey. Yeah," he whispered, grinning. "I know." Slowly, he lowered his mouth to hers and kissed her. A promise of sorts, of things to come, once he straightened his employee situation out.

"I'll be back."

"Okay. And, Bru?"

"Yeah?"

"Hurry."

Oh, man. Staring at her teasing expression, he groaned. Why did he have to deal with his crew, now, of all times?

Bru opened his eyes as he slowly regained consciousness. *What the devil had he run into?* he wondered foggily and glanced up at his surroundings. How had he gotten into the cabin's kitchen? And why was he sitting at the kitchen table? Head throbbing, he attempted to cradle his head in his hands, only to discover his hands were tied behind his back.

"So. You're awake."

Dully, Bru allowed his gaze to follow the sound of the familiar voice. Jim. As he stared at his scowling ranch hand, Big Daddy's words echoed in his mind. *"We've heard tell of rustlers in the area."* Rustlers. Yeah, Bru thought, that would explain the menacing look on Jim's face and the fact that his head felt as if it had just been strip-mined.

Racking his brain, Bru tried to remember the "five fool-proof ways to win people over to your way of thinking." Because, for the moment, they were the only weapons at his disposal. Make eye contact. That was one of the rules, wasn't it? Yeah. Eye contact.

Sighing, he looked Jim square in the eye and tried to reason with him. "Look, Jim, if you think you're going to get away with—"

Irritated, Jim took a swing.

Contact.

"Augghh!" Bru winced at the stabbing pain that seared through his eye. Man, that hurt. He blinked and shook his head. Okay. So much for eye contact. He shifted in his seat, trying to find a more comfortable position. But it was tough, being tied up and all.

"Shut up," Jim hissed.

"Yeah," Jim's sidekick, parroted, "shut up."

"Shut up, Donny," Jim barked. "Both of ya just shut up. I can't hear myself think." His gaze swung to Bru. "You talk too damn much."

Yeah, well, be that as it might, he didn't have much choice, Bru thought sourly. His gun was in his saddlebag, and with his hands strapped to the chair this way, the only thing he had going for him was Penelope's advice. More flies with honey. Uh-huh. Right. She'd never had old Jim-boy here for a student. But, he figured, exhaling heavily, what else could he do?

"Listen, Jim," Bru began, trying to swallow his fury and inject a conversational—nay, friendly—tone into his voice, "cattle rustling is a pretty serious crime in these parts. I'm sure that once you've had a chance to think—"

Another right cross to the jaw from Jim. "I said, shut up!"

"What are we gonna do with him, Jim?" Donny asked.

Bru's eyes swung to Donny. He recognized him from the Bar None up the road. So, he thought with a sigh, it was an inside job. Great. Briefly he wondered if any of his other hands were involved. He doubted it. So far, it looked like it was just this less-than-dynamic duo.

His pulse picked up speed as his thoughts turned to Penelope. Thank God he'd left Penelope outside. Hopefully, she would figure out what was happening, and stay out of sight. The idea of her stumbling into this situation unawares struck terror in his heart.

"I don't know. I ain't figured that part out yet." Agitated, Jim dropped into a chair and began to nervously bounce his leg. "They were all supposed to be out in the back section the whole week, about an hour's ride from here."

"Ya gonna kill him?" Donny wondered.

"I don't know," Jim snapped. "I told ya. I ain't got that far."

"I'll do it," Donny volunteered. "Can I, Jim? Huh?"

Bru's eyes widened as he watched Donny make a bid to be his executioner. From an image standpoint, he wondered what tack Penelope would take with this particular knucklehead.

Penelope glanced at her watch again. Bru had said "a few" minutes. She'd heard him. Throwing a pleading gaze to the cloudy sky, she had to wonder if she was doomed to spend the rest of her life waiting for him. Most likely, she thought, her mood becoming as dreary as the weather. She wanted to get inside. She wanted to dry off. She wanted a cup of coffee. She wanted to warm up.

With Bru.

Sighing in disgust, Penelope slid off Lightning's back and tied him and Burrito to a nearby tree. Of course, she didn't want to seem presumptuous by just barging in, she thought, picking her way from puddle to puddle as she headed toward the lovely, rambling, ranch style "cabin." So, she would go to the back door and listen. She wouldn't intrude. She just wanted to find out what was taking so blasted long.

She moved to the cabin door, but the shouting inside stopped her from entering. Nervously peeking into the window, Penelope froze, and gaped at what she saw. Bru was tied to a kitchen chair? But why? And why were the two men hitting him?

The gun. She needed...she needed...she needed the gun. Penelope's knees were knocking so badly, she was afraid they would be able to hear them back at the house. Surely this was some kind of bad dream, she thought, her mind whirling frantically as she rushed back to Lightning, dug into Bru's saddlebag and pulled out his revolver. A .357 magnum ought to do the trick.

Rustlers.

The word echoed ominously in her mind. Big Daddy had been right, she thought, fumbling with the holster strap. There were rustlers out here. Bad men. And if what she'd seen was any indication, they were very bad men. Okay, the gun was out of the holster. Now what?

Lightning nickered.

"Shh," Penelope cautioned, glancing up at the horse. "Easy, old boy."

She needed to heed her own advice, she thought frantically, trying to still the tremors in her hands. But, heavens to Murgatroyd, she was not prepared for this. She wasn't good at this kind of emergency. She knew how to handle social emergencies. She knew how to win friends and influence people. She didn't have the first idea how to…to… How had Bru phrased it? she wondered as she checked the gun's cylinder for bullets. Oh, yeah, kick some butt.

Not loaded. Uh-oh.

Digging into the saddlebag, she finally located a box of bullets. Okay, good. How hard could this be? She'd seen Bru do it a dozen times. Fumbling, she tore the top off the box. Six bullets left. More than enough. There were only two guys in there. She'd have bullets to spare, she thought crazily. All righty. Hands trembling, she tucked the gun under her arm and tilted the box. The six bullets slid out of the box and, one at a time, landed in her palm, and then, as if in slow motion, they bounced off her palm and landed in the puddle at her feet. All, that is, except one.

"Oh, no!" she breathed, staring dumbfounded at her one remaining bullet. *Relax, regroup, relax,* she chanted to herself. Gracious. Dropping the bullet into a random hole, Penelope snapped the cylinder shut and closed her eyes and hoped for the best.

"Ready or not, here I come." She gritted it out through clenched teeth and, tossing her soggy tresses over her shoulder, marched on wobbly legs to the house to kick some cattle-rustling butt.

Silently, she moved around back, until she found another entrance to the cabin. Thankfully, this back door was unlocked, and she quietly crept inside, through several rooms, toward the sound of angry voices.

Peering through the opening in the kitchen door as it stood ajar, Penelope held her breath and tried to get a handle on the proceedings and, at the same time, bring her body under control. Nearly paralyzed with fear, she stood rooted to the spot, her only movement the violent trembling of her hands. Tightening her grip on the revolver's handle, Penelope exhaled slowly. As quietly as she could, she pulled the hammer back and, with both thumbs, cocked the gun.

Click.

"What was that?" Jim demanded, his head snapping toward the origin of the sound.

Penelope's heart stopped beating.

"What was what?" Donny wondered.

"Knock it off, you idiot," Jim growled.

Leaning against the wall to steady herself, Penelope peered through the crack in the door at Bru, and sagged with relief. He was still alive. *Thank God, thank God,* she murmured silently. She didn't know what she would do if anything ever happened to him. Probably cease to exist, she thought, feeling suddenly desolate at the thought of life without Bru. She couldn't lose him now. Especially not now that she realized how much a part of her he'd become.

Taking a deep breath, she narrowed her eyes, and pursed her lips. It was up to her to help him.

"We gotta get out of here." Agitated, Jim strode to the kitchen counter, grabbed his gun, and leveled it on Bru. "Okay, Mr. Brubaker. We gotta go. Donny's gonna gag you, then I want you to come along real nice now, and don't give us no grief. Got that?"

"Are we gonna kill him yet?" Donny asked, looking vaguely disappointed.

"I told ya. I ain't got that far yet," Jim barked. "I'll know when the time is right. Now gag him, Donny."

As Donny found a linen kitchen towel and fashioned a crude gag over Bru's mouth, Penelope decided that it was time to take action. She knew from various self-defense courses in her life that once the victim went away with the perpetrator, the chances of his survival dropped considerably. And Bru would survive, or her name wasn't Penelope Grace Wainright. Taking a deep breath and sending up a prayer, Penelope pushed the kitchen door all the way open and strode boldly into the center of the room as Jim and Donny worked on Bru's gag.

Eyes bulging, Bru stared at her from the captivity of his kitchen chair. *Run, Penelope! Get out while you have the chance!* his expression warned.

Shooting him an off-kilter smile that was meant to instill confidence, Penelope, hands shaking violently, took aim. Bru squeezed his eyes tightly shut. Perhaps if she pretended they were bean cans she would be all right, she thought, and sent up a prayer that she wouldn't accidentally hit Bru.

"Drop your guns, bean cans!" she barked, the loudness of her voice startling even her.

Bru's brows shot skyward.

Taken by surprise, Jim and Donny spun around and stared at her, then exchanged glances, trying to determine if this little gal was serious.

"Bean cans?" Donny asked.

"I'm *serious!*" she shrieked, slipping her finger over the trigger, and in her enthusiasm she accidentally squeezed it. The shot resounded throughout the kitchen, blowing off Jim's hat and exploding a teakettle in the process.

Bru's wide-eyed gaze flew to Jim, then back to Penelope.

"Oops." Penelope sighed, staring at the gun in her hands.

Bru frowned.

"Damn," Jim breathed, fingering his bare head with the hand that wasn't holding his gun.

Donny began to whimper.

"I said put the gun down, and I mean it. *Now, dirtball!*" she shrieked. Tossing her bedraggled hair over her shoulder, she eyed them and sniffed loudly. She'd never felt so alive and in control in her life. Perhaps she would think about giving up image consultation and become a cop.

"Okay, okay," Jim said, setting his gun on the sink, "just don't kill us."

"I don't know if I will or not," Penelope retorted. Her stance wide, she swayed back and forth on her legs. "I ain't figured that part out yet. Now—" Jeering, she motioned with the revolver "—on the floor, hands behind your back. Both of you."

"Yeah, okay. Just be careful with that thing," Jim snapped, looking with wary eyes at the gun that wobbled in her hand.

Within moments, Penelope had both rustlers lying face-down, on the floor and, stripping the scarves from around her neck, she was tying very professional-looking knots at their wrists and ankles. Rushing over to Bru, she hurriedly untied the ropes that bound him and pulled the gag from his mouth.

"Oh, Bru!" she cried, falling into his lap and wrapping her arms around his neck. Frantically she kissed his cheeks, his nose, his jaw, his forehead. "Oh, Bru, I was so scared," she breathed, babbling, laughing, crying with relief.

Framing her face in his hands, Bru stilled her fluttery movements and looked deep into her eyes. "Penelope." He breathed her name reverently and kissed her mouth. "Thank God you're okay." He kissed her again, then pulled away and studied her face, drinking her in. "You are without a doubt the most amazing woman I have ever known."

"I am?"

Hugging her tightly, he nodded, burying his face in her neck. "Uh-huh." He sighed. "What am I going to do with you? Then again—" he groaned, tilting her face to his "—what am I going to do without you?"

Chapter Eleven

"What did they say?" Penelope wondered. She watched as Bru put the cordless phone away on an antique desk situated near the fireplace. Striding across the beautifully furnished Western-style living room, he dropped onto the couch next to Penelope. In the hour since they'd tied up the rustlers, they both had a chance to shower and put on some clean shirts and jeans they'd found in one of the bedroom drawers.

His smile was weary as he slid his arm across the back of their seat behind her shoulders and regarded her. "Mac said to stay put. They left the chuck wagon in the camp section and they all rode toward the main house several hours ago. They only just now got back. They say the road to the house is flooded in some areas, and the water's still rising, so we can't drive back. Big Daddy say's he'll arrange for one of his helicopters to come get us when it's not raining quite so hard."

Penelope nibbled her lower lip as she rolled up the cuffs of the roomy pair of jeans she now wore. "Are you sure

Jim and Donny are going to be all right locked in the cattle truck?''

Lifting his hand off the back of the couch, Bru stroked her cheek. "Hey, is my little Calamity Jane going all soft on me now? Come here." Slipping his arm around her shoulders, he tugged her over next to him and fingered the damp tendrils of her soft, shiny hair. "Don't worry about those idiots. They have a roof over their heads, and four lovely metal walls to stare at. And after I'd unloaded the cattle, there were even several places where there wasn't too much manure for them to sit. What more could they want?''

She smiled. "You're right."

"Have I thanked you for saving my life yet?"

"Several times."

"Only several times? That's not enough."

His upper lip curved into that smug curl that never failed to jump-start Penelope's heart. As he pulled her across his lap and lowered his mouth to hers, she felt the familiar tide of passion begin to sweep her out to sea. Buoyant from the sensations that nearly obliterated all rational thought, she coiled into his embrace, and tried to forget what they had just been through. Tried to lose the horror of nearly losing him. The very thought had her tightening her arms around his neck, frantically returning his kiss, desperate to connect with him, to make him understand how much she needed him.

Breathing raggedly, they explored with their mouths, tasted, and attempted to impress upon each other emotions for which there were no words. However—try as she might to let herself go, to enjoy this time alone with the man who'd somehow managed to make her see the world in a whole new light—she couldn't. For there, deep in the niggling recesses of Penelope's mind, she realized that even though on one level she'd saved the day, on another level she'd failed him.

And she'd failed Big Daddy.

And in a way, by allowing herself to become involved with a client, and breaching that sacred trust, she'd failed herself.

A groan, deep in Bru's throat, rumbled in her ear. Shifting slightly, he pulled her more firmly onto his lap, and leaned her back against the couch's armrest. Her body reacted, even as her mind screamed for control. She couldn't do this. She couldn't lead him on this way. It wasn't ethical. Besides, she thought dismally, she knew she wasn't the kind of woman Bru dated, and she never would be.

"No, Bru," she whispered, her voice tortured, as she pushed at his chest and struggled to sit up. "Stop. Please." Her eyes were filled with tears and her voice was broken.

Obviously dazed, Bru blinked up at her. "Everything okay?" he asked, concerned. Reaching toward her, he tried to grasp her arm. But she was too fast, and his hand landed on his thigh. "Penelope? Honey? What's wrong?"

Moving away from him, she pushed herself off the couch's overstuffed cushions, got to her feet and crossed the living room to the knotty-pine entry door. She needed to think. She couldn't think straight with him looking at her that way.

"I...I...I don't know Bru. I have to think. I can't think. I need to—" she waved a hand, misery welling up in her throat as she tried to explain something she didn't understand herself "—think."

Dazed, Bru watched her pull open the big pine door and slip outside, into the pouring rain. What happened there? he wondered. One minute, they were setting each other on fire, and the next—he stood and walked to the giant plate-glass window—she was standing in the front yard, in the pouring rain. Running his hands up the window casing, he leaned against the sill. For a long moment, he watched her doing battle with a demon.

Most likely, he thought, blowing a long heavy breath that fogged the window pane, a demon named Bru. She was probably standing there wondering why she'd allowed him to kiss her that way. After all, she could never love a lost cause like him. And could he blame her? He'd gone out of his way to make her life miserable from the moment she arrived. What a joke. Well, the joke was on him, because not only had his father won the war, so had she.

He'd been beaten. Thrashed. Brought to his knees by a briefcase-toting image consultant. Funny thing was, he'd never been happier. At the same time, he'd never been more miserable.

He was in love with Penelope. And he was getting the sickening feeling that it wasn't mutual.

Minutes ticked by as he stood there vacillating, wondering what to do. He was such an emotional wreck all of a sudden that he barely recognized himself. Why was he acting this way? he wondered in disgust. He'd never been so fearful of a challenge in the past. No. In the past, when he saw something that he wanted, he'd gone after it.

"Go get her," he thought to himself. *"You can do it. Project the image you wish to achieve,"* he muttered, quoting Penelope, as an emotional momentum built deep in his belly. Man, he thought with a self-deprecating grin, she'd really done a number on him. Pushing off the window casing, Bru strode to the front door, suddenly full of purpose. He hadn't felt this passionate about anything since…since he ran his father's empire. And even that paled in comparison to his feelings for Penelope.

Descending the front stairs, he stepped out into the rain and, coming up behind her, placed his hands on her shoulders.

"Penelope, sweetheart, we need to talk. Come on in out of the rain."

Ignoring his plea, she drew a ragged breath and turned to face him. "Oh, Bru. I've failed." Lifting lashes laden with drops of rain and tears, she looked plaintively up at him. "I shouldn't be kissing a client," she whispered.

His heart ached. Had he caused the agony in her eyes? If that was the case, he would spend the rest of his life making it up to her. He sighed. "Penelope, won't you forget the professional thing for ten seconds and just be a person?"

"I *can't!* Don't you see?" she cried. "I have *failed.* Wainrights never fail."

Dragging a hand wearily over his face, Bru rubbed the water from his own eyes. What she was trying to say, but was too blasted polite, was that she saw him as a failure. But that was only because, up till now, that had been how he wanted her to see him.

Well, he decided, giving his head a clearing shake, he would just have to change that now, wouldn't he? Bru, like his father before him, never let anything worthwhile slip away, and he wasn't about to start now. He would do anything for Penelope. Hell, he'd round up and count the stars, if she asked him. And if need be, he thought—feeling suddenly filled with dogged determination—he would work side by side with his interfering father, in these last years before the old man was actually ready to retire, if it would make his Miss Prim happy. Yes! He could do that. For her. And, amazingly enough, he also wanted to do it for his father and...himself.

"I've been thinking about going back to work for my father, down at Brubaker International," Bru suddenly heard himself saying. He held his arms out to her, to catch her when she leaped into his embrace.

"No!" she shouted, her expression vehement.

"No?" This was not the joyous response he'd expected. Slowly, he lowered his arms to his sides.

"Nooo!" she cried. She was blubbering now, as she planted her hands on her hips. "You can't do that! You're too happy out here, on the ranch. It would be wrong to force you into something you don't want to do. I'd feel responsible if you went back, and you'd only end up hating me." Dropping her hands, she brought her tear-filled eyes to his troubled ones and sighed heavily.

He shook his head. "No, Penelope. I could never hate you. In fact, I lo—"

She cut him off. "Bru, you don't need to change, don't you see? You're perfect. Just the way you are."

"But, Penelope, if you would just listen, I'm trying to tell you that I lo—"

"No buts." She placed her fingers over his mouth. "I mean it. I love you, just the way you are."

She loved him? That was his line. His ears began to ring, and his knees went weak. Had he heard her correctly? His heart surged with joy. Could it be? After everything he'd done to drive her away, she loved him? It was a miracle! He wanted to climb up on the cabin and shout his happiness from the rooftop.

Eyes flashing, he searched her face for the truth. "Truly?" he whispered and, reaching out, drew her against his chest.

Sighing, she nodded her head and gave him a rueful smile. "Truly."

"Aww, Penelope," he said, the raw emotion thick in his throat. Locking his arms at her waist, he rocked them to and fro. "Me too, honey. Me too."

The rain, beginning to abate now, was a fine mist as it wafted out of the sky, soaking them both to the skin once again. Neither of them seemed to notice, as they stood in front of the sprawling cabin, clinging to each other for dear life. Bru kissed Penelope's temple, inhaling the floral scent of her, enhanced by the summer rain. In a nearby puddle, a bird twittered and flapped, enjoying the impromptu bird bath.

"What makes you so sure that I wouldn't be happy back at my old job?" he murmured, holding her close.

She drew a shuddering breath. "Because you said…"

"In the past, I've said a lot of stupid things. Prideful things." He sighed. "But this last week, and especially this afternoon, a lot of things have come into focus for me. My priorities suddenly sorted themselves out. My father is right. There is nothing more important on this earth than family." Gently, he squeezed her. "And I know I still have a lot to learn from that man. What better way than to go back to work side by side with him?"

"Well, actually, he won't be th—"

"Shh, let me finish." Cupping her head in his hands, he pulled her cheek against his shoulder and stroked her rain-soaked hair. "Penelope," he began, wondering if she could feel the brutal way his heart was pounding in his chest, "I'm serious about family. I want one of my own. Sooner than later."

She went perfectly still in his arms.

Oh, well, he thought, deciding to damn the torpedoes. He had to tell her sooner or later, and it might as well be now. "And when I think of my future children, I think of you as their mother."

"Me?" she squeaked.

He smiled and rested his chin at the top of her head. "Yes. You. And if you can stand a stinker like me for your husband, I want you to marry me. As soon as possible. I love you, Penelope Wainright."

Leaning back in his arms, she looked up at him.

"Never, in all my life, have I ever been more serious about anything." He grinned at her. "Back there, with Jim and Donny fighting over who was going to knock me off, my life kind of flashed before my eyes. And, to be perfectly honest, I didn't like much of what I saw. Only the parts where I was with you meant anything at all."

"Oh, Bru," she breathed, looking up at him in awe.

"Marry me, Penelope."

"Yes," she said, suddenly giddy with delight. "Yes! I'll marry you!"

Laughing, Bru swept her up in his arms, and spun her around, and clung to her, full of joy, and relief, and hope.

"What's so funny?" Penelope asked, smiling, as he let her slide along his body till her feet touched the ground.

For the first time since she'd known him, the stress in his face had eased.

"You remind me of my mother."

"What's so funny about that?"

"Nothing. It's great. Really. It's just that I've finally gone and done it."

"Done what?"

He shrugged sheepishly. "I've finally turned into my father."

Giggling, Penelope squinted up at him. "Oh, no. You're much taller."

Hooting with laughter, he kissed her cheek.

"Besides," Penelope said, snuggling up against his chest, ignoring the steady drizzle that plastered their clothes to their bodies, "I adore your father. Of all the people you could pick to emulate, he's one of the best."

"Well, one thing is for sure," Bru said, holding her tight as he walked her back toward the house. "When we get home, I'm going to shake his hand."

"Why?" she asked as they reached the porch steps.

"Because he brought me the most wonderful woman in the world." Lifting her up into his arms, he carried her up the steps and paused in front of the big pine door. "I love you, Penelope."

"I love you too, Conway," she teased, looping her arms around his neck and angling her mouth to his for a kiss that had him weak in the knees.

"You know, I like the way that sounds when you say it." His gaze locked with hers. "Hey," he whispered, "I've gotta get you inside, and out of these wet clothes."

"Yeah, yeah, I've heard that line before." She laughed at his wounded expression.

"I promise you. No more lines. No more parties, no more wine, women and song. Unless, of course, the wine and song are with you." His mouth curved devilishly, bringing his dimples out of hiding.

"I always knew it would end this way," Penelope said

saucily as her husband-to-be carried her across the threshold.

"Oh, yeah?" Bru's laughter wafted back out to the front porch as he gave the old pine door a closing shove.

"Yeah," she teased, beaming up into his face. "Wainrights always get their man."

"Surprise!"

The lights snapped on as what sounded like a cast of thousands—but was in reality only the Brubaker clan and a few dozen close friends and neighbors—shouted and clapped. A three-piece ensemble struck up "For He's a Jolly Good Fellow," and the partyers began to blow on, and whirl, their noisemakers.

Dumbfounded, Penelope and Bru stepped into the gaily decorated living room, through the columned archways just off the grand foyer, and into the festive hubbub. Having just exited the helicopter after being airlifted from the cabin and still wearing their damp clothes, they blinked in surprise at each other.

Looking curiously around, Penelope tried to piece the puzzle together. How had everyone gotten here in this weather? Trust Big Daddy not to let a little thing like a flash flood interrupt his plans. "What's going on?" Bru murmured, pulling his future wife close to his side. Pasting a broad smile on his face, he nodded at the crowd of well-wishers.

"I'm not exactly sure." A tiny frown marred her own practiced smile. Why had they shouted, "surprise" at her and Bru? All the signs and banners on the walls read Happy Retirement, Big Daddy! or Congratulations, Big Daddy! Slowly, Penelope shook her head. Shouldn't they all be yelling at Big Daddy? Eyebrows high, she glanced up at him and lifted her shoulders.

Rushing forward, Big Daddy tackled them both in his effusive embrace. "Are you surprised?" he cried.

"Uh..." Penelope stammered and exchanged glances with her fiancé. "Yes, actually."

"Hot diggity!" He chortled and rubbed his hands together. "It was the little woman's idea to toss a little retirement party together and surprise you two this way."

Grabbing their arms, Big Daddy tugged them through the throng of friends and family, toward a small stage someone had fashioned in the middle of the living room. Nudging the dazed pair up the stairs and onto the platform, Big Daddy tapped and blew noisily into the microphone. The ensuing screeches of feedback finally had the crowd turning their attention to the commotion on the stage.

"Everybody, hesh up! Y'all hear? Hesh now! Can I have your attention?" Big Daddy boomed to the folks who had gathered to celebrate.

Fumbling for Bru's hand, Penelope looked around in confusion, and was grateful for the steadying arms that circled her waist and squeezed. The milling throng began to settle down, and she felt her eyes widen and a smile steal across her face. Was that her mother near the wall, beaming proudly up at her from her wheelchair? And—her breath caught in her throat—Aunt Geraldine was here, too? And Randy! Already she could see that he and Bru's youngest brother, Hank, had formed a friendly alliance. Amazed, she scanned the crowd. Over in the corner were Fuzzy and Chef and Red, their weathered faces all wreathed in smiles. Mac and Buck stood near the door, arms folded across their broad chests, watching the proceedings in amusement.

"Big Daddy," Bru said in a quiet aside to his father, a puzzled frown on his face. "What's going on? All the banners say, Happy Retirement. Why are they all yelling at us?"

"That's the surprise," Big Daddy told him in a stage whisper. "I'm really retiring. For good. The end. Kaput. You get the idea. We knew that there was probably nothin' that would surprise you more than that," he cried gleefully, and slapped his knee. Laughing at their expressions, the older man turned to face the crowd and adjusted the microphone close to his mouth.

"For those of you who don't already know her, this little lady standing next to my oldest son is his image consultant, Miss Penelope Wainright, of the Wainright Image Consulting firm. Aside from my retirement, today we are celebrating the fact that she and Bru brought down the rustlers that have been plaguing our spreads over the past few months."

Penelope felt heat rush into her cheeks as the neighboring ranchers sent up a jubilant cry. She glanced up at Bru, who was sporting his typical easy grin.

Big Daddy continued. "But that's not all. Oh no! We are also here to celebrate Penelope's success at taming the beast—" he paused and waited for the good-natured catcalls and applause to die down "—and Bru's return to the helm of Brubaker International." Hesitating, Big Daddy turned and squinted up at his oldest son. "You are returning, aren't ya, boy?"

"Are you really serious about retiring?" Bru tightened his grip around Penelope's waist.

"Yep."

Bru's grin turned skeptical. "Well, it wouldn't matter if you were or not. I've been planning to come back for a while now."

Reeling, Big Daddy clutched his son's shirtsleeve to keep from falling down. "Really, son?" he whispered, tears of joy filling his eyes.

"Yep. And that's not all," Bru said, good-naturedly parroting his father's earlier words. His lip curling lazily and his dimples appearing deep in his cheeks, he reached forward and adjusted the microphone to his considerably taller height. "I have an announcement of my own to make," he said, and drew Penelope back into the circle of his arms.

A hush settled over the audience.

The loving look he bestowed on her had Penelope's heart soaring wildly. As she gazed back into his eyes, she knew beyond a shadow of a doubt that she belonged with this man for the rest of her life.

"Just an hour or so ago, Penelope Grace Wainright—" Bru turned his fiancée to face him and cupped her cheeks in the palms of his hands "—agreed to become Penelope Grace Brubaker. My wife." With a look so full of love it stole the breath from the collective sea of onlookers, he brought his lips to hers for a tender kiss.

Beaming and hooting, the gathering roared its approval. Penelope's mother pressed her hands to her mouth in happy wonder.

Jaw slack, eyes buggy, Big Daddy stared up at them. After a stunned moment, his eyes rolled back in his head and—without warning—the shocked Brubaker patriarch fell over backward and landed on the impromptu stage with a thud. The guests gasped.

"Oh, my land!" Miss Clarise rushed to her emotional husband's side. Mac and Buck were hot on her heels, and Penelope and Bru hovered at her side, exchanging worried glances. "Big Daddy?" Miss Clarise patted his face until his opened his eyes and squinted up at her. "Big Daddy, are you all right?"

"Yep." Big Daddy groaned and, accepting Bru's help, stood and looked adoringly up at his son's fiancée. "Nevah bettah." Tiptoeing, he planted a loud kiss on Penelope's cheek. "Welcome to the family, honey pie. It would be my honor to give you away at the weddin'." His eyes were shiny with unshed tears.

"Thank you, Big Daddy," Penelope whispered, her throat tight, her heart full to bursting for the man who'd already given her the gift of a father's love.

As he turned back to his wife, Big Daddy's rubbery grin overtook his face. "Well, darlin', now that we've got Bru all squared away, I guess we can stop fussing ovah him and start concentrating on Mac."

Buck slapped Mac on the back and hooted with laughter. "Hear that, brother? Big Daddy's gonna start concentrating on you."

Sighing in futility, Mac shook his head. "Yeah, well, don't get too cocky. Remember—when he's done with me, you're next."

Abruptly, Buck stopped laughing. "Uh-oh."

"Yeah." Mac grinned. "Uh-oh."

Epilogue

Two Months Later

"Well, Big Daddy," Miss Clarise murmured as her husband whirled her enthusiastically around the dance floor, "I have to hand it to you."

"Why is that, sugar lips?" Big Daddy puffed, his energetic footwork leaving him pink-cheeked and more than a little winded. Ever competitive, he was trying to outdance his oldest son and his new bride at the young couple's wedding reception.

It was a beautiful Saturday in early September. The outdoor wedding was—as all Brubaker parties and gatherings tended to be—a roaring success. Hundreds of friends, neighbors and family members had assembled to observe the holy exchange of vows taken by Penelope and Bru in the beautifully decorated gazebo near the rose gardens, and then partake of the sumptuous fare and do a little visiting and dancing at the reception. And though the guests all seemed to be having an excellent time, no one was having more fun than Big Daddy.

"Slow down some, and I'll tell you!" Exasperated, Miss Clarise finally stopped dancing in the middle of the large parquet dance floor that had been set up on the rolling lawn, and waited for her diminutive husband to samba his way back to her.

"Tell me, sugar lips," Big Daddy gasped, gripping his wife around the waist and dipping her dramatically toward the floor. "But don't evah expect me to slow down."

Giggling, Miss Clarise rolled her eyes and patted her hair back into place as Big Daddy hauled her into an upright position and began steering her around the floor.

"Oh, Big Daddy, you are something else." Her eyes glowed with the love she felt for her husband of over thirty years. "And though I probably shouldn't tell you this, you were right about Bru needing to find a wife and settle down. It's so obvious how much he loves Penelope," she mused, allowing her shining eyes to stray over to her son and his new wife as they moved around the dance floor together. Penelope's eyes were radiant with joy as she looked up into Bru's adoring face. Miss Clarise grew suddenly misty. "I don't think I've ever seen a more devoted husband."

"Ahem." Big Daddy hiked a competitive brow, a rubbery grin pushing his cheeks and eyes into a wreath of wrinkles.

"Present company excluded, of course," Miss Clarise amended with a gentle smile.

The music changed, becoming slower. Softer. Following suit, the folks on the dance floor adjusted their steps and moved closer together.

Fluffy white clouds floated gently in the endless blue sea of the Texas sky, and a light breeze lifted the curls at her brow, bringing with it the scents of autumn. The dance floor was packed with people young and old, talking, laughing and humming along with the tender lyrics of the love song the orchestra played. Off to the side of the gazebo, in a special pond built especially for the wedding, a pair of swans paddled in lazy circles.

All in all, it was probably one of the most beautiful, memorable days in Miss Clarise's life. And not just because of the elaborate decor, the local symphony or the imported champagne. No. None of those things could equal the love and happiness she experienced in the arms of the man who held her close.

Big Daddy tightened his grip at her waist and whispered into his wife's soft, graying hair. "Remind you of our wedding day?"

"Seems like only yesterday."

"Mmm," Big Daddy nodded dreamily. "And before you know it, we'll be dancing at Mac's weddin'. Mark my words."

Miss Clarise reared back in her husband's arms and looked warily at him. "Big Daddy," she asked, a warning note tingeing her voice, "what in heaven's name have you gone and done now?"

"Just a little surprise." His eyes sparkled with mischief. "But I can tell you this much right now. That boy ain't gonna know what hit him."

* * * * *

Big Daddy might be planning Mac's wedding, but the head of the Brubaker family is going to be in for quite a surprise. For Buck is about to fall for
HIS BROTHER'S INTENDED BRIDE.
Don't miss the next enchanting installment of
THE BRUBAKER BRIDES,
coming in December from Silhouette Romance.

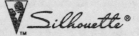

Take 4 bestselling love stories FREE

Plus get a FREE surprise gift!

Special Limited-time Offer

Mail to Silhouette Reader Service™

3010 Walden Avenue
P.O. Box 1867
Buffalo, N.Y. 14240-1867

YES! Please send me 4 free Silhouette Romance™ novels and my free surprise gift. Then send me 6 brand-new novels every month, which I will receive months before they appear in bookstores. Bill me at the low price of $2.67 each plus 25¢ delivery and applicable sales tax, if any.* That's the complete price and a savings of over 10% off the cover prices—quite a bargain! I understand that accepting the books and gift places me under no obligation ever to buy any books. I can always return a shipment and cancel at any time. Even if I never buy another book from Silhouette, the 4 free books and the surprise gift are mine to keep forever.

215 BPA A3UT

Name	(PLEASE PRINT)	
Address	Apt. No.	
City	State	Zip

This offer is limited to one order per household and not valid to present Silhouette Romance™ subscribers. *Terms and prices are subject to change without notice. Sales tax applicable in N.Y.

USROM-696   ©1990 Harlequin Enterprises Limited

SILHOUETTE WOMEN KNOW ROMANCE WHEN THEY SEE IT.

And they'll see it on **ROMANCE CLASSICS**, the new 24-hour TV channel devoted to romantic movies and original programs like the special **Romantically Speaking-Harlequin® Goes Prime Time.**

Romantically Speaking-Harlequin® Goes Prime Time introduces you to many of your favorite romance authors in a program developed exclusively for Harlequin® and Silhouette® readers.

Watch for **Romantically Speaking-Harlequin® Goes Prime Time** beginning in the summer of 1997.

If you're not receiving ROMANCE CLASSICS, call your local cable operator or satellite provider and ask for it today!

Escape to the network of your dreams.

ROMANCE CLASSICS

Daniel MacGregor is at it again...

New York Times bestselling author

NORA ROBERTS

introduces us to a new generation of MacGregors
as the lovable patriarch of the illustrious MacGregor
clan plays matchmaker again, this time to his three
gorgeous granddaughters in

THE MACGREGOR BRIDES

From Silhouette Books

Don't miss this brand-new continuation of Nora Roberts's
enormously popular *MacGregor* miniseries.

Available November 1997 at your favorite retail outlet.

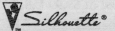

1998

SUNDAY MONDAY TUESDAY WEDNESDAY THURSDAY FRIDAY SATURDAY

Keep track of important dates

Three beautiful and colorful calendars that celebrate some of the most popular trends in America today.

Look for:

Just Babies—a 16 month calendar that features a full year of absolutely adorable babies!

1998 CALENDAR
Just Babies
16 months of adorable bundles of joy!

Hometown Quilts
1998 Calendar
A 16 month quilting extravaganza!

Hometown Quilts—a 16 month calendar featuring quilted art squares, plus a short history on twelve different quilt patterns.

Inspirations—a 16 month calendar with inspiring pictures and quotations.

Inspirations

A 16 month calendar that will lift your spirits and gladden your heart

Steeple Hill™

◆ HARLEQUIN®

Value priced at $9.99 U.S./$11.99 CAN., these calendars make a perfect gift!

Available in retail outlets in August 1997.　CAL98

DIANA WHITNEY

**Continues the twelve-book
series 36 HOURS in
September 1997
with Book Three**

OOH BABY, BABY

In the back of a cab, in the midst of a disastrous storm,
Travis Stockwell delivered Peggy Saxon's two precious babies
and, for a moment, they felt like a family. But Travis was a
wandering cowboy, and a fine woman like Peggy was better off
without him. Still, she and her adorable twins had tugged on
his heartstrings, until now he wasn't so sure that *he* was
better off without *her*.

For Travis and Peggy and *all* the residents of Grand Springs,
Colorado, the storm-induced blackout was just the beginning
of 36 Hours that changed *everything!* You won't want to miss a
single book.

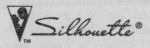